Fur Coat & No Knickers

An acclaimed collection of short stories & poems by award-winning author

ADRIENNE VAUGHAN

Wishing you the best of everything,
Adrienne Vaughan. x

www.adriennevaughan.com

First Edition

Original artwork: Reta Wrafter © 2016

Cover design: John Reddy www.paintbox.ie

Author photo: Peter Alvey Photography www.alveyandtowers.com

ISBN: 978-0-9955689-07

Contents

Books by Adrienne Vaughan

Available from Amazon

The Hollow Heart

A Change of Heart

Secrets of the Heart

And coming soon …

Scandal of the Seahorse Hotel

Dedicated to Harry Wrafter

(October 1933 – October 2015)

Teacher, hero, Dad.

We miss you.

Praise for Adrienne Vaughan

'The story-telling has the same charm and magic I've always found in a Maeve Binchy.'

Elaine G (Top 100 Amazon Reviewer)

"Brilliant, clever, engaging – so many emotions! A wonderful read from a superb writer, who never fails to delight."

Margaret Kaine (Author)

"This book will tug at every heartstring, evoke every emotion and fill your thoughts."

Sharon Booth (Book Blogger)

"Beautifully written, gripping yet with great warmth between the pages. I loved it!"

June Tate (Author)

"A brilliant storyteller, another five star read, prepare to be swept away!"

Lizzie Lamb (Amazon #bestselling author)

Introduction

I have always been a huge fan of the 'Short Story' – especially classic little tales that stay with you long after reading and often imparting more of an impact than even the most lauded novel. Compiling this collection has been fascinating for me, because these stories were written at very different times in my life. The earliest first penned in the mid-eighties and my latest, just last month.

Next Door's Business was published in the *Sunday People* supplement *Love Sunday*, *The Adventuress* was highly commended in the Romantic Novelists' Association's Elizabeth Goudge Competition and *A Seed of Doubt* appeared in Debbie Flint's 2014 compilation *Hocus Pocus*.

Rereading *The Messenger*, this feels like my attempt at a homage to some of the great Irish writers I was introduced to at Goldenbridge, my convent school in

Dublin, namely Brendan Behan, Frank O'Connor and W B Yeates among others. And the vintage flavour of *Fur Coat & No Knickers* and *Heir Apparent* – written many years apart – are clearly reflective of my ongoing love affair with P G Wodehouse.

The Retiring Type is based on an email character – Gertrude, a cross-dressing psychiatric nurse – who my dear friend, Anna Bergmann, always asked after whenever we wrote via this relatively new-fangled medium, and my mother reminded me about *A Married Man* – which she read many years ago – saying it was so chilling she could never forget it!

The poems are a real mixed bag. I write little verses all the time. I even wrote for a greetings card company once, so it's a habit hard to shake. The only influences I can cheekily claim are Dorothy Parker, Emily Dickinson, Marc Bolan, David Bowie and maybe a bit of Pam Ayers. All my novels come with a free poem, by the way.

I do hope you enjoy this little selection of odds and sods and I'd love to hear from you, especially if you'd like to find out more about my writing. You'll find me at adrienne@adriennevaughan.com or on Twitter @adrienneauthor – let's catch up soon.

The Visit

Come, come in and sit. The fire is lit.
The chair pulled close, the flame to kiss your face with peat breath.
Give, give me the coat. Scarf from the throat,
So you can feel soft heat on skin, and sink into an easing of the day.

Here, an amber sip. Caress the lip.
A brush of oil on timber. Sweet the scent of bread, turned fresh to toast
Glistening with the melt of gold,
For you to taste, and keep the hunger from your flesh.

Don't speak. There is no need.
You look so weary from the world of words.
Don't move. The merest smile, flash-lights the room
And bathes my very soul in sunshine.

So timeful stands the clock, upon the shelf, it's always there
Its face a threat benign, above the gentle glow of hearth

Which draws the seconds in, absorbs
the minutes of
The precious, treasured hour you spend.

The cat, who knows him well, will take his
rising as her cue
To curl around his legs and tango, purring to
the hall
To take her leaving for the night,
along his side.
They're like for like, the cat and he.

The door is softly closed. I press my hand
against the pane,
To hold the essence of you in. The
bloodless fingers of the dead.
Then turn and face the room. Now
monochrome. An airless tomb.
All colour drained away. An artist's
wash, of grey on grey.

And see, where you have sat, an empty
hollow hogs the chair.
And I feel hollow too. Is there a draught
from somewhere?
Just an echo through the heart.
And still the embers burn. Until the visitor's
return.

George & Mildred

George was excited and ran the entire length of the barge tail wagging wildly; something of a feat considering his arthritic hips. Sneakily, he had navigated the gang plank, climbed aboard and trotted below deck before Faith had even noticed he had gone.

She had been sitting quietly in her usual spot watching her swan, an ethereal creature which had been living a solitary life on the Grand Canal at Foxton Locks for over a year. She visited often, sitting entranced as he smoothed through the water, leaving other wildfowl bobbing in his wake, ignoring all attempts at engagement with humans afloat or ashore. She fancied he knew she was there, admiring from a distance, his elegance all the more striking because he was just one, alone. He somehow soothed and calmed her, reassuring in his aloneness, affirming her solidarity, making her singleness noble. He never came close,

George saw to that, although she always had food in her bag to tempt him. Today he was resting in a reed bed on the far bank, bathed in sunlight, a halo of mist around his bowed head.

She hotched up on the bench, catching her jacket on the metal plate bearing the inscription 'Brian Formby, 1946 – 2014'. She felt the snag in her sleeve, glaring at the insouciant plaque. Two words, two dates, but no explanation of who Brian was or why the bench was dedicated to him; could they not have stretched his legacy to another few words?

'Brian Formby, 1946 – 2014, late of this parish, boatman and conservationist. In recognition of his lifetime of service to the upkeep and preservation of the canal and waterways.'

She could picture the little ceremony unfolding at the water's edge. The bench gleaming with newness, reflections dappling its smooth oak surface; a wreath of May flowers tossed into the lock, bouncing as it burbled away. One of the boatmen played a shanty on an accordion as the garland floated onwards. Brian's passing respectfully acknowledged in a small, soulful gathering. If only it had been like this. But it had not. She had gone to stay with her sister, near to breakdown and when she returned the bench had been erected. A tribute yes, but cold and impersonal and so bland – no tribute at all, really. She hated the bench, if she were honest, but the lure of the lock was too strong.

She adored the canal, the merging of the waters, the travellers converging, the adventure, the romance.

"Is this your dog?" a commanding voice boomed. Faith and the swan looked up. A mop of white hair, bushy eyebrows and bright eyes appeared above the deck of the barge. George was under one arm and an almost identical George under the other.

"Which one?" she called back, equalling his volume; she had had to speak up a lot more lately. She stood, straightening to her full five feet, dragging her bag onto her shoulder.

"This cheeky young pup." He nodded at George. "The other cheeky young pup is mine." He indicated the wriggler trying to lick him.

"I'm sorry." Faith collected herself. "Was he causing trouble? I didn't notice. I was …"

"I know, day dreaming. Nice spot for it. Do it all the time myself, day dream-aholic me."

"Not really." Faith was practical, down-to-earth. She had to be, had for a long time. She pulled the lead from her pocket and moved to re-capture George, who was settled in the man's arms, occasionally reaching over to sniff the other George. She took George from him averting her eyes. The doors were thrown open and she could see remnants of detritus scattered about the cabin.

"I'm sorry. If there's any damage…"

"Not at all." The booming voice again, vaguely familiar. "Only joshing with you. Time for a coffee? Just made a pot."

Faith was flustered. He jumped off the gang plank and held out his hand.

"Lionel Flynn Maguire. Pipe you aboard ma'am?" He smiled into her face. White teeth, could be false; manicured moustache; paisley cravat; pale blue shirt; tan leather waistcoat and jeans. Too old for jeans she considered. Nice looking though.

"Sorry just going." Turning away she accidently dropped the lead and George, lithe as a puppy, sprang onto the gang plank and disappeared after the other George. The man laughed, making no move to help recover the errant canines.

"They've made friends. Can't we?" Hand still extended. Big, strong hand. She took a deep breath.

"Faith Fornby. You've already met my dog George."

"Your hand's frozen. Why don't you stay for a coffee? I won't bite I promise. Can't say the same for Milly, though." He tilted his head, acknowledging the playful growling below.

The barge was surprisingly roomy and beautifully furnished, once the dirty dishes, glasses and discarded clothing were ignored. He bade her sit, the table before them highly polished, with a bright brass rim attached. The porthole curtains were beautifully made and there were sumptuous matching cushions scattered over rich velvet seats. Charts and seascapes adorned the walls and behind a glittering collection of decanters, two luminous portraits in black and white dominated one wall. One, obviously her host as a young man and the other an elegant cream-skinned beauty, wearing an off-the-shoulder satin gown, diamond droplets and an upswept coiffure, evening gloves, arched eyebrows, a perfect mouth looking back over her shoulder, coquettish and alluring. Faith gasped.

"Vivienne Ventura, the actress." She moved closer. "And you, I thought I knew you, Lionel Mack. Of course we've never met, but when someone is as famous …"

"*Was* as famous." He came into the salon with mugs. "Please don't say you're a huge fan."

"I won't." Faith gave him her first smile. "Loved her, thought you were awful."

His laughter made the boat rock.

She could not believe she had accepted his invitation, she had never had dinner on a boat of any kind. Brian, not a strong swimmer, had always avoided water. It was she who loved the canal, she who had instigated and insisted on the connection to the locks, fascinated by its history, immersed in its present and longing to be part of its future. It was a magical place to her. And then, after the accident … well, anything adventurous was totally impractical. It was so difficult to do anything that required manoeuvring him, not just the wheelchair but the entire container full of accompanying paraphernalia.

Somctimes she would be eaten with guilt at not making the effort and would bundle them all up –Brian, George, the wheelchair and the entire mobile A&E department – to take them somewhere, anywhere, just to say she had, show she could. But it took such an effort and so much time. Once there – a deserted park in November, a bleak beach in March – they would eat a limp sandwich, drink cold tea, turn around and go home. Remarking on what a great time they had and they must do it more often. They never did though.

They were welcomed aboard again. This time George had been bathed, reluctantly brushed and Faith wore perfume. Lionel had lit candles and Milly flashed a collar of rhinestones. He took the wine graciously, despite the supermarket label, placing it on one side and then taking champagne from an ice bucket, poured skilfully, expertly holding a napkin around the bottle. Faith wriggled, straightening her skirt, longing to kick off unfamiliar heels; the champagne kicked in instead and soon they were chatting easily, enjoying the shared remembrances of people the same age.

"When did Brian pass on?" asked Lionel, slicing cheesecake.

"Eighteen months and two weeks on Thursday," she replied immediately. "Vivienne about five years ago?"

"Eight years, four months and two days."

"When will that stop, I wonder?"

"What?" he asked topping up her glass.

"The automatic timer." She gazed into space.

He sipped brandy, indicating for Faith to slide round beside him. She pushed neat grey locks behind her ears, fiddled with her necklace.

"I don't normally drink. I'm sure I'm tipsy. Couldn't drink really. Always had to drive if we ever went out. Mind you, I couldn't get the wheelchair up the ramps in the end, Brian was too heavy. No social life at all really. People stop ringing after a while. I don't blame them. Everyone has their own life to lead, their own 'wheelchairs'. Bloody lonely though."

He patted her hand on the table.

"That's why I bought the barge. No friends left – not real friends anyway. Thought if I was going to be on my own, I might as well get out and about under my own steam. No point staring at the same four walls, and with Milly for company what more do I need?"

Faith flicked off the shoes, tucking her feet under her. "Why no friends, a rich, famous couple like you?"

He went to pour another drink. Faith put her hand over her glass. George and Milly shifted on the rug, snuggled together dozing.

"Mildred had a drink problem."

"Mildred?"

"Vivienne was a stage name. We were Lion and Milly at home. She drank. Not much to begin with but then more and more, all the time. Hiding bottles, telling lies." He glanced at the photograph. "So beautiful, so wicked, so sad."

"You named the dog after your wife?"

That laugh again. "No, I met this Milly at the rescue centre, fell in love with her, and when I heard her name, it had to be. Always be a Milly in my life."

Faith smiled, watching him look tenderly first at the picture and then at the little dog. "Vivienne retired early, I remember. It was a shock, height of her career. Just stopped."

"Had to." He held his glass aloft.

"And you? You stopped too."

"Mainly to keep an eye on her. She was living way beyond our means, running up debts, having fine wines delivered from Selfridges, ordering new gowns, furs. Living in fairyland really." His beautiful booming voice had become a whisper.

"Poor Lionel." Faith's head was on his shoulder. He took her chin in his hand, lifted it and kissed her softly on the lips. She smiled and kissing him back wrapped her arms around him, pressing his body against her. He reciprocated her embrace and they sat entwined. The blare of the taxi horn pulled them apart.

George and Milly were barking. Lionel poked his head above deck; there were headlights on the road above the towpath.

"Shall I send him away?" he asked softly.

Faith had not slept wrapped in a man for over twenty years, nor had she ever experienced the lullaby of the water. She opened her eyes slowly, savouring the exquisite pleasure of both newness and familiarity.

"I've never been unfaithful," she said.

"We're both widowed. Parted from them now," he said into her hair. She closed her eyes, giving herself permission to enjoy being desired.

She was not surprised when she returned the next day and the barge had gone. The empty berth gave a better view of the canal. Scolding herself for a dull, seeping disappointment she had no right to feel, she sat down on Brian's bench. George sniffed along the towpath, seeking out a new paramour to pursue.

Breaking through the back water, her swan glimmered into view, twirling effortlessly in the slipstream, arching his neck to dip his beak in the water, sweeping his head upwards, a prism of diamonds spraying the air. She nodded in greeting. He came closer. She laid her offering of food on the water, taking her seat again. He tilted his head and looked her straight in the eye.

"I'm not going anywhere," she told him, as sensing the dog's return he moved effortlessly away. George re-appeared, tail wagging with mischief. "Fresh from another brief encounter, no doubt." She gave George a wry smile, pulling up her collar against the wind, as they started home together.

A blast, like a fog horn made them jump, as an engine came chugging through the water, the barge homing into view.

"Where are you going?" he called in that gorgeous enunciated voice.

"Home," she said, though she was smiling.

"But you promised."

Milly ran to the bow of the barge, gruffling at George. He tugged on his lead, pulling Faith back.

"What do you mean?" She had been wrong-footed, assuming he had gone. The blurry badinage of the night before had dissolved, only a soft ripple in her memory.

"You said you'd come, spend a few days. Drift about a bit."

"I couldn't possibly." She made to go, flustered.

"You said you would, fair maid," he called loudly,

hands placed in an extravagant gesture on his hips. He had been a musketeer after all.

"I'm sorry." She had been rather tipsy.

She walked on, she was nearly back at the bench. She turned to look at him, standing her ground, watching him carefully.

"I didn't think you were serious. Were you?"

"I went to stock up. You said you like porridge, strawberries … oh and more champagne."

He drew the barge into the mooring. There was a commotion behind in the reed bed, wings beating as feathers ruffled. They turned to look. Her swan was not alone. Another swan had appeared, not too close but close enough. Neck arched regally, Faith's swan circled away, not too far, then turning he swam back, back to the new swan. They watched the elegant courtship for a while, entranced. The swans settled.

"It's only a little holiday, plenty of berths, you can take your pick …" His booming voice tailed off, not quite as confident now.

Faith thought for a minute. She could phone her neighbour. She would keep an eye on the house. Clothes, toiletries? He read her mind.

"I've everything here – washing machine, dryer, borrow anything you want." There was a slight plea to his tone.

Faith did not have an impetuous bone in her body.

She could never, ever be described as impulsive. Giving herself a little shake, she released George's lead. The dog ran to the boat and leapt aboard. Tail wagging furiously, he looked back at her, eyes alight.

By now, Lionel was grinning broadly, holding out his hand, his eyes were shining too. She stepped aboard.

Satisfied, George trotted off in search of his chum. They were soon stretched out on the deck, noses almost touching.

"I hope you've plenty of dog biscuits," she told him, placing her hand next to his on the tiller.

"Plenty of everything." He gave a cheeky grin. "Don't you fret, milady."

She started to laugh, really laugh. It sounded so odd. She had not laughed like this for so long.

"You always were a dreadful actor, absolutely awful," she reminded him.

Still grinning, she half-closed her eyes, watching as the water sparkled. It bubbled gaily as they powered through the slatey blue. He was staring straight ahead, guiding them past the other boats, one hand on the tiller, the other around her waist. She leaned into him and looking back saw that the swans had emerged onto the water, graceful necks arched as they swam not quite together but a short, tentative distance apart.

End

Carrying a Painting

Oh, you're an artist! In awed exclamation.
Not a bus driver! A flawed occupation.
I dabble, that's all – I reply with a sigh.
Oh no, it's a gift, you must have an eye.
Two as it happens but neither spot on,
Quite blurry in close up, the outline not strong.
Is that why you're here, to sketch landscapes
and such?
Who me? No, not really, a rest pretty much.
It's wrapped up quite tightly, I wish I
could see.
I bet you are famous. Be wasted on me.
Someone once mentioned they saw talent there.
But to me it's well hidden, barely a flair.
Well, original art is quite priceless, you know.
So 'handle with care' and mind how you go.

I carried the picture onto the flight
And the crew checked my ticket
As you'd guess that they might.
Then showed me my seat, the entire front row.
And the art sat beside me – its own little show.

Next Door's Business

Flo was deep in conversation with her sister, her weekly call. Sometimes she had to think hard what to talk about, her life was so bland compared with Lily's. Lily had been a dancer, worked in Vegas, then on the cruise ships. Married an Italian late in life, although he ran off with a sax player, and now lived in Little Venice — Lily, not the Italian. But there had been 'goings on' next door and Flo had been saving the news all week.

"Well, I knew it was him straight off. Could tell by his tone, all shouty and pompous-like. And I said to Poldark, listen to it calling the shots, telling her do this, do that. How she puts up with him I'll never know. Time she gave him the elbow. Been going on far too long, and no further on with it either, if you ask me.

"Echoey?" Flo listened. "I'm in the kitchen, on my mobile. You said I needed a new phone, one with a volumiser. Must be the reception. What was I saying?

Oh yes, she never does, you know, ask me, I mean, doesn't speak to anyone really. Proper 'home bird' Mother would have called her. Gets her hair done in the high street mind. Never seen her in the same outfit twice, always beautifully turned out."

Flo gave her hair a fluff.

"Definitely got a bit of Marilyn Monroe about her, though my Bill preferred Diana Dors, more patriotic, he said, preferring Diana. Showed he wasn't going to be swayed by no Yank piling it on with a push-up bra and a bottle of peroxide. Well, he'd have known being in the war and all that."

Flo listened again, then replied.

"Well, the Suez Canal then. Scary enough I'd have thought. Weren't the Americans there? I'd never be blonde myself. Mother said it was common. Remember when my Bill brought that wig home with the stockings? What on earth was he thinking?"

Flo laughed, Lily had remembered.

"Oh yes, he gave you the wig, I'd forgotten. Did you get the stockings too?" She fiddled with flowers in a vase; they needed a dust. "I'm in the parlour now, moving into the sitting room. Not a mobile? Of course it is, I'm swishing around all over the place."

She went to the window.

"Anyway, I digest … Oh, you know what I mean. Sometimes I'd see her having a bit of a sun bathe in the garden — she'd speak then. 'Not too much noise last night was there Mrs Aldwich? Sorry if we went on a bit,' she'd say, but I never complained or let on I heard anything. Such a lovely girl, and you're only young once. 'Nice to hear a bit of life,' I always said, and it is, if I'm honest. Days can be very long with not much happening. Ah, cordless, is that it? Well it's marvellous. I'm on the landing. Where was I?"

She took a few breaths; the stairs were steep.

"Sometimes she doesn't go out at all. Not that she's on the social — too up-market for that. Probably on the computer all day doing goodness knows what. Young Brad told me I should get on the he-mail myself when he came to put the phone in. You'd like him, good-looking boy, twinkle in his eye too. He says to me, 'Mrs Aldwich if you were a couple of years older I'd run away with you.'

"Brad says he-mail does everything nowadays, shopping, pays the bills, puts money in your bank, all sorts. Not for me though, I never learned to type, couldn't bear an office. You know, it's like a flippin' typing pool in the library these days. No one speaks or even looks up. Charming, no point going there for a bit of company.

"Anyway those computers get viruses so best keep away. I told you the flu jab never agreed with me, brings my veins right up.

"There it goes again." She held the handset aloft. "No, not my washing machine finishing its spin, her phone – I'm at the back door. Goes a lot. I can hear sometimes, when the window's open. Not the actual words but she has a sweet voice, softly spoken, purring almost. You can see why she gets rung up so much, sounding so caring all the time.

"Doesn't use the phone when he's there though. All you can hear is him yawping on at her, until he either falls asleep or drops down dead drunk. Shouldn't have said that really, but I've noticed lots of stuff in the recycling bin, and not just beer — expensive booze, proper champagne and gin from India in a blue bottle. Well that's not your Co-Op specials is it?

"I'm sure it's not her. Takes too much pride in her appearance to get bloated with drink, and if you ever see his face — which is rare — he's always rushing to that big car with his head down, talking into his mobile, looks a bit ruddy and pock-marked if you ask me. Funnily enough he always seems to whisper into his." She looked at the handset. "Are you sure this isn't a mobile? I was going to put it in my handbag in case you rang when I'm at the bingo. Well, he whispers into his when he's coming or going, which is odd for such a noisy beggar.

"Mind you, the house must be spotless. Mrs Granger comes three times a week and her old man does the garden, windows and whatnot. I've never liked them much, you know who I mean, live by the church, keep themselves to themselves, bit snobbish for a couple who only do cleaning and maintenance but she seems to like them well enough. Been with her since she moved in and that's eighteen months now.

"I don't know, eighteen months and still no nearer to settling down. Comes and goes as he pleases, anytime of the day or night. Saying that, if he does stay the night he leaves very early, before I even let Poldark out, and I'm an early riser as you know. I don't miss many worms. Though I don't sleep well these days and those pills make me groggy. It's no wonder I don't take them as often as I should … I'm in the bedroom now.

"Anyway, I digest. So the last thing I heard, which you would because of his big, bossy gob, was him, shouting, furious, saying he'd been betrayed. Called her lots of names and told her it was over, all the benefits and everything else that went with it. Benefits, I thought, who gets the benefit of a lovely girl, warm, clean home and other attentions, if you take my meaning.

"Then I heard her pleading and the sound of her crying, and a bit of crashing and banging about, and then the door slammed. I looked out thinking it was him storming off in his big flash car, but no, it was her, barely dressed and out in the cold night, no bag, no suitcase, no nothing. She staggered down the path and held onto the gate for a minute, sobbing and catching her breath. I couldn't see her face in the dark but she had her hand to her cheek.

"There was a bit more smashing about in the house, so I lifted Poldark off the windowsill, closed the curtain and turned off the light. You don't want neighbours knowing all your business, do you? Anyway, it all went quiet and by the time I let him out in the morning the car had gone too."

Flo went quiet, letting the impact of it all sink in. Lily was impressed, she could tell.

"But here's the thing. It wasn't until Brad came back to show me how to get this going." She was interrupted. "So I can talk and do things at the same time — no dear, I'm nowhere near a boiling pot — that he asked about her next door. He said he knew the telephone was being disconnected and probably investigated and I said she wasn't the type not to pay her bills but he certainly was. And Brad said she was an ex-worker — so they must have been colleagues at one time — and he'd called on her after they got talking in the garden. No dear, you are funny, he definitely said ex-worker. Anyway, told me she was rather 'high maintenance', whatever that means … oh, and not a natural blonde. I told him nice boys don't look, but it made me wonder if they got a bit friendly… well he's much nearer her age. Anyway, perhaps that's what set her chap off, Brad being there …

"… hang on, what's that? It's banging dear, in the garden. Well I never, a For Sale board and someone taking pictures. He didn't hang about, oh no, his house. Brad said he paid all the bills, has quite a few properties around the town, so Brad told me. Well, he did carry on as if he owned the place. Ought to have heard him. Be a bit quieter now I suppose.

"No, no, dear, not in the bathroom, definitely not. I wouldn't take the mobile in there. That doesn't seem decent somehow, talking on the phone when you could be … well anyhow … and this is such a nice neighbourhood. We're all proper around here dear, as you know."

End

A Pink Day

Today has been a day of Pink
No making beds or kitchen sink.
It's been a day of turquoise sea
And greenish fields of greenie gris.

It's been a day of vivid blue
Lapis laz in every hue.
It's been a day with silv'ry bits
And golden sun through eyes like slits.

A day of vibrant, livid reds
Of sunlit boats and sun-tan beds.
The sort of day the sun god sent
Free of guilt and free of rent.
A day that makes you stop and think
A glorious day, in shades of Pink!

The Lemon Bag

It was a monumental decision, the biggest decision she had ever made and it filled her with dread. And then looking at the bag she felt a little heartened; lemon is a good colour, bright and positive. Hopeful.

She zipped the bag closed and pulled the handle out sharply. Its yellowness shone beacon-like in the hall as she struggled past the rusting bicycle and grimy milk crate, taking her last black sack to the bin. She pushed aside the other tenants' spillages with her boot — a pungent mix of teabags, peelings and stale beer — victoriously depositing her detritus atop the pile in the bin. The lid wouldn't close but it didn't matter, not her problem anymore.

Freewheeling the lemon bag behind her, she noticed Mrs O'Driscoll watching from the window on the third floor and giving a little smile of knowing she nodded. She waved back brightly. No hint of where she was going. No mouthing "See you later." Not this time.

It was drizzling. She took a taxi to the station, relieved the cabbie was not chatty, choosing instead to be an opinionated intellectual who talked to the radio, agreeing as Melvyn Bragg's guest denounced a great artist's entire body of work.

She was tired of other people's opinions; she had heard enough. Retreating into her bubble, she placed headphones in her ears and listened to The Cure on her iPod; the song was one of her 'Desert Island Discs', an unusually jolly, plinky-plonky tune for that particular combo. She closed her eyes and found herself sitting on a beach, under a palm tree for the entire journey, glancing just once at the lemon bag, reminding her of sunshine.

Checking the station clock, a huge octagonal art deco time-piece, she was reminded of another time: meeting under a clock, a date to watch a movie, maybe a musical or even better to go dancing. She had worn a floaty yellow dress, twirling in her mind's eye as she was propelled from the past back to the present.

Clutching water from somewhere in Italy she clambered aboard, suddenly very thirsty — a thirst for what, she wondered? Freedom, perhaps.

She had been here before; so many journeys into the unknown and now she just didn't know. Panicking slightly, there was still time to get off, go back. She looked left and right.

A man in the same carriage lifted the yellow bag effortlessly onto the rack above. She blushed her thanks. He gave her a big, soft smile, warm as sunshine, and misgivings melted as the bag shone too, perched over her head like the sun.

Rattling north from London, the whole of England passed unseen outside the window as she slept, the first sleep in months, in years it felt. Eventually the train swooped around a curve of coast, edging into a town that gazed defiantly across the North Sea. Borders had been crossed.

She could barely remember if she had phoned, given a time? Relieved, she spotted her friend jogging along the platform to greet her. Her friend hugged her so tightly, her bruised arms hurt again, those dark purple bruises still sharp with the pain of memory.

"My God," her friend exclaimed. "I hardly recognised you, you look so …"

Worn out with it all, she thought but didn't reply.

Instead her friend took the lemon bag. Wheeling it towards the car, she hauled it heavily into the boot.

"What on earth have you packed? Anyone would think you'd left home." Her friend grinned, then frowned as the penny dropped.

"It's new. I should have picked a lighter one." She

gave the bag a wink as she closed the boot.

"And such a bright colour, not desperately practical," her friend said with a laugh in her voice. "Just like you not to think things through."

"Oh, I've thought things through alright," she replied, pulling the sun visor down as they turned out of the car park. There was a break in the cloud.

End

Another Time

What other world is this I've seen
Twixt then and now, and in between?
What shaft of light, revealed a crack
Of somewhere else, of time gone back?
What slice of life, that's gone before
Was glimpsed beyond an open door?
How can the stranger, I've just met
Be someone known, I can't forget?
Familiar, warm, yet fresh and new

I wonder if you felt it too?

Did you feel the slightest shake?
Not lightening flash, or earthy quake
But just a nod, the merest blink
A half heart-beat, held on the brink.
An instance in a glance we saw.
That we had been and loved before.
Who were we then, what had we known?

That this life has not hid or shown?

The archer's aim struck straight and true,
A searing flame, turned red to blue.

Flecks through the eyes I'd come to know
Another place, quite long ago.
A breath away, we stand apart.
What finished then, should never start.
What's now is here and it should be.
Your now is you. And mine is me.

A captured moth, the memory holds
Releasing as the wings unfold …
Then let it free, we need not fear
Such other worlds exist, it's clear.
Lost souls entwined, as yours and mine
Can be as one … another time.

Heir Apparent

The family had been wealthy when he was a child, and he was destined to be affluent again — though whether this was because of the trust fund, to which he often referred or the fact that one of his many business deals was just about to come to fruition, was never quite clear. But Laurence was never very clear about anything, and this was probably one of the endearing characteristics that had attracted me to him in the first place.

I remember him standing, resplendent in a mossy tweed jacket, mustard waistcoat and jeans, leaning languidly against the bar in a very unfashionable city centre pub. And it wasn't very clear whether he was with the people close by or waiting for someone to join him.

He intrigued me immediately. He looked so beguiling, gaunt and frail and somehow mysterious, a poet from another era I mused as he smiled, watching me struggle from the bar with two gin and tonics and an obscene cocktail contraption for Marlene – it was happy hour. He offered to help, extending elegant fingers gracefully towards me and Laurence became part of my life from that moment on.

He never actually asked me out. Laurence didn't do that sort of thing – go out or ask — the first because he seemed to be always out, probably because he didn't appear to have anywhere in which to stay. And the second because Laurence never asked for anything. He just took. Very delicately and unobtrusively but he just took, nonetheless.

I found him, later that evening, after our initial encounter in that awful pub, leaning in what I now know is his time-honoured style against the window of the vintage clothes shop I manage. I had returned to check the back door. I didn't trust Marlene, and I was right. Laurence, however, caught me off guard.

"I followed you. I hope you don't mind." He smiled dazzlingly, producing a prefect rose bloom of palest pink from behind his back and thrusting it at me.

"Yes, I do mind," I replied, but my eyes belied the statement and I melted, thinking this was all rather romantic and, having had very little romance in my life thus far and being therefore susceptible, with hardly a murmur of protest, felt I had no choice but to succumb. In less than ten minutes we were in another, slightly better bar, sharing a bottle of wine, which I'm sure I must have paid for, now I come to think of it.

On reflection, I did vaguely notice that, although at first glance Laurence appeared debonair, his shoes were badly scuffed and the cuffs of his jacket a little frayed. But he had beckoned me so intriguingly to follow him along the street that I did. And from that moment on, if I'm being totally honest, this was to be the basic pattern of our relationship. Laurence beckoned and I followed.

He didn't really move into my tiny, one-bedroom apartment on the south side of the city, he just seemed to be there more and more frequently as the weeks progressed.

"I'm in transit," he said, by way of explanation, making vague movements with his hands when I asked where he lived early on in our acquaintance.

But I wasn't really bothered. In truth I was glad of him. Having recently undergone a particularly painful breakup, I'd severed all previous ties and moving to a new area, fresh start and all that, had been piteously lonely ever since. Laurence was a welcome respite.

Still it wasn't until his razor had become a more or less permanent fixture in the bathroom that I decided to confront him with the fact that, although it was indeed a pleasure to have him around, two could not live as cheaply as one and he was currently a non-contributory member of the household.

Soft brown eyes became instantly moist as he gazed at me across the breakfast table, his spoon held mid-plunge above the expensive muesli he insisted was the only thing he could stomach at such un-godly an hour.

"Oh, darling, it pains me so for it to be like this. You just can't imagine. Everything seems to be against me lately. Two deals I'm working on are taking forever to come through – but they will, I swear it. And then, the sky's the limit. We'll buy a house, take a holiday, whatever you want, it's yours." He squeezed my hand. "With you in my life I feel as if I can achieve anything. You're my rock."

He brightened considerably after this outburst and tucked into his breakfast with relish and I was briefly mollified. Laurence was very convincing.

"Any news about the trust fund?" I asked on another occasion, pushing the electricity bill pointedly towards him.

"Trust fund?" He put his glass of vintage port to one side. "Ah, the trust fund, yes. Well, when that particular boat comes in, we will be flying high. Icing on the cake to my mind."

"Isn't thirty-nine a little old to still be waiting for such a thing?" I was clutching at straws. He smiled at me indulgently, as if he found my ignorance of the ways of old money quite endearing.

"You may not believe this, my angel, but I was a little reckless in my youth, so father's left the money in trust until I'm forty. Wily old devil my dad is – was, I mean. Don't worry though, only eight months to go, and we'll be 'on the pig's back' as they say."

I glanced at my watch; I was going to be late for work. Laurence went back to his newspaper. He'd taken to having the *Financial Times* delivered, said he liked to keep an eye on the market. I kissed him briefly, not a little perturbed at his lack of concern over the impending state of the household accounts, and grabbing my brolly grumpily ran out into the rain. But when I glanced back at the first-floor window, I spotted a huge sign being held aloft by a kimono-clad male. It was Laurence, and the sign read 'I love you, hurry home!' Besotted I stood blowing such fervent kisses at him and the sign that I missed my rotten bus.

Laurence considered himself rather artistic and told me he had studied in Paris, though the trauma of being torn from public school – when his father had gambled and finally lost the family fortune – had apparently contributed to the fact that he had virtually no qualifications to speak of.

His accent, rather more Watford than Windsor, was, he told me when I enquired, because his governess had insisted he adopt a more colloquial tongue in order to survive and succeed in the cruel world of commerciality. Amazing foresight for a tutor, I considered, to envisage that Laurence's father would lose all their money and the heir apparent would have to make his own way in the big, wide world.

"Yes, amazing," Laurence confirmed, promptly changing the subject and insisting I accompany him that very evening to The Salon, a project allegedly so dear to his heart he was astonished he had never mentioned it before.

The Salon, was not as you might expect, the place where Laurence's flowing locks were trimmed and tamed and, on closer examination, expertly highlighted, but rather a rambling terraced house off the South Circular Road, which Laurence presented as a haven for writers, artists, poets and musicians. A commune of like minds and unfettered imaginings, where ideas, opinions and creative genius combined to create the artistic masterpieces of the future.

We stepped over the rusting pushbike and old cooker in the hallway to be greeted in the sitting room by a pale but none the less bubbly Rastafarian called Marvin. After much hugging and back-slapping, Laurence introduced me through clouds of incense and marijuana smoke, and as it dissipated I discovcred there were quite a few bodies in varying positions of repose scattered about the room.

"Long time no see, man," said Marvin, grinning toothily at Laurence. "We got food in de kitchen, if ya wan' some."

Laurence was grateful but declined the invitation to dine. Marvin shrugged and gave him the once over.

"Ya new woman, she feed ya good." And indeed it was true, Laurence had certainly filled out quite a bit in the short time I had known him. In fact to such an extent, his limited wardrobe was beginning to creak at the seams.

A boy in faded denims and a severe haircut waved vaguely in our direction.

"Wayne!" exclaimed Laurence warmly. "Your new work, how's it coming along?"

The boy called Wayne picked up a piece of paper from the littered floor and Laurence motioned for me to sit. I perched precariously on the edge of two old beer crates, wishing I hadn't worn my most expensive two-piece as Marvin handed me a can of warm Red Stripe, kindly pulling off the ring top for me. Laurence smiled encouragingly at Wayne, who cleared his throat noisily and began …

"It was all around, the noise of silence.

Dressed in the bottle blue of death and decadence.

The children were ripped apart with their apathy,
Mothers crying. Afraid of the dark.
Aching with hunger,
Bring the pigs to the slaughterhouse."

A silence followed. Marvin and Laurence looked with pride at each other and then reverently at Wayne.

"Awesome, man," Marvin said.

"Well done, the boy wonder!" Laurence seemed genuinely moved. "I can see how you're really benefitting from this environment, Wayne. How long before you feel you'll be ready for a recital?"

Wayne shrugged, drawing deeply on an oddly shaped cigarette. A wailing screech pierced the stillness. I jumped, convinced some poor moggy was being strangled, but then the sound softened and I realised it was music, a strange neo-Japanese cacophony emitting eerily from another part of the house.

"That's Yikoshi," Marvin told Laurence. "He's working on a new concept. Gonna be global, I can just feel it."

Laurence nodded wisely. "I totally agree. Just amazing isn't it?" He said to me.

"Amazing," I answered, and indeed I was amazed.

We left The Salon an hour later armed with a clutter of oddments Laurence said was his equipment but which looked like a bag of battered shoes, a bundle of sheaf music and an old portable typewriter. We had stood transfixed at Marvin's demented paint splatterings, read Wayne's *other* poem and kissed two toddlers in the crèche, which looked like it could easily double as a garden shed. It had been a long evening.

We walked home. Laurence had managed to extract my last ten pounds from me as a donation towards the upkeep of the place. Whereupon Marvin overcome with joy, offered me one of his paintings, and although Laurence urged me to accept – surely an investment – I felt obliged to decline. How could I deprive a true art lover of one day enjoying a work of such rare quality? Marvin appreciated my selflessness.

It had started to rain and my purse and my patience had been stretched. Laurence was nothing if not sensitive and guessed by my silence the evening had not been the success he had hoped. Pulling me into a doorway he tried to soothe me, kissing me hotly and telling me he adored me because I had been so serene and undaunted in the presence of such overwhelming talent, and I was indeed, in his considered opinion, a true patron of the arts.

I remember looking at him, smiling shiny-faced beneath the lamplight and wondering how someone could be nearly forty years on the planet and still be so innocent, so naïve and, at times, so bloody irritating.

Laurence didn't work like other people worked. And he wasn't unemployed in the genre of the masses either. He received no benefits I was aware of and seemed to spend most of his waking hours – usually from noon onwards – strolling around the town seeking out this person or that in a rather aimless and disorganised fashion.

I bought him a couple of new outfits, no longer prepared to tolerate that when his meagre ensemble was at the cleaners he tried in vain to either get into my clothes or just lolled moodily about the flat in my kimono. His fortieth birthday approached, and although on more than one occasion I mentioned he did appear a little older than his reputed thirty-nine years, his response was to just gaze wistfully into the distance and cough painfully, extolling the virtues of modern medicine in the face of the evil tuberculosis.

The day before his birthday Laurence was in celebratory mood. He told me that as luck would have it one of his deals had just come off and he was taking me out to dinner to celebrate as indeed the very next day we would be rich and I'd never have to work or worry about money again. I adored him like this.

We dressed in our finery and went out on the town. We dined at a pretty French bistro, drank gallons of wine and ended up in a ritzy, downtown nightclub, dancing and laughing together, so in love and without a care in the world.

Laurence made plans. He told me how he was going to invest his money, taking his rightful place in society and would become an influential industrialist just like his father before him. He made my heart swell; he seemed so determined to restore respect and honour to the family name. I remember him looking at me earnestly, those deep, beautiful brown eyes glistening with love and hope.

"You've seen me through the bad times, darling. I'll never forget that. And now that I am to become somebody, I finally feel I have the right to ask you if you would do me the honour, nay the privilege, of becoming my wife."

I almost gagged on my drink. This was indeed a new Laurence. Marriage, he always told me, was just an outmoded and unnecessary encumbrance, an arrangement he appreciated suited some but not him. It was not a contract into which he could ever consider entering, being a free spirit and all that. So I was more than a little surprised at the proposal and perhaps should have been more suspicious than I was.

Of course I accepted, kissing his sweet face, and we taxied home laughing to make love by candlelight.

As we lay spent and happy on the floor in the sitting room much later, Laurence kissed me tenderly and then tottered into the bedroom. I followed, curious, and found him piling his belongings into my only leather suitcase.

"What are you doing?" I was bemused.

"With the dawn, my sweet I go to claim my fortune. Father left my trust find in the hands of our bankers in Jersey. I've to travel there tomorrow to sign the papers and release the money. There's no need to be concerned. All proper and above board."

He stroked my hair.

"I'll come too," I announced, reaching for my holdall.

And then he surprised me, telling me firmly that he would prefer if I didn't. The bankers had known the family for many years. He didn't want them to think he had suddenly acquired a fiancée to help him spend his fortune. He was adamant they would meet me when I was his wife and could afford me the respect I deserved.

"How long will you be gone?" I asked him.

"Not too long, I hope. I've to go to London first. The release forms will be with the family solicitor. Then the boat to Jersey. I'll have to take the ferry, cheapest route of course." He continued with his packing. My brain started working overtime.

"I've an idea. Why don't I give you the money and you can fly to London and then onto Jersey? It'll be much quicker and you'll arrive in a style befitting your station."

"Oh no, my darling. I couldn't possibly. I'll be fine on the ferry, providing the weather's not too bad, of course."

In all the time I had known him, he had never actually taken hard cash from me. He'd wheedled money out of me for various projects and had lived rent-free that was true. But he had never, ever succumbed to the temptation of using me as a bank.

"No, no darling, please. I don't want your money."

"It's not my money. It's our money. We're practically married, aren't we? Take it, Laurence, please. I'd be much happier if you did."

He sighed, hugged me tightly and asked how much I had stashed away. The sum total of three thousand pounds, I told him proudly, lodged in a building society – my dream cottage in the country was still a long way off.

"Okay, write me a cheque for three thousand, I know where I can cash it quickly and make sure the money from the building society is in place to cover it," he said with remarkable monetary dexterity for one so artistic. "But" — and this was his piece de resistance — "to show good faith, take this cheque and lodge it in your bank account too. That way everything's more than covered."

He reached inside his new Barbour – a birthday gift from me – and withdrew a piece of paper, another cheque, made out to him for the princely sum of ten thousand pounds. It was post-dated two weeks into the future.

I gasped. "I don't understand?"

"I told you one of my big deals came off. It's nothing, pocket money. I'll just sign the back. Take it, it's yours." He kissed me. "Insurance, my darling. Plenty more where that came from."

Flabbergasted, I promised to sort out the financial arrangements the following day, insisting he had a good night's sleep, he had a long journey ahead of him. I was beside myself with excitement while Laurence of course, slept like a baby.

When I awoke the next morning Laurence had already left. It was the earliest I had ever known him to waken. He had taken the car – I'd recently managed to secure a loan on a second-hand Renault, following Laurence's assurance a change in our circumstances was imminent – and set about organising our finances as agreed the previous evening.

Three weeks later, I found myself sitting in that unfashionable pub, with my sales assistant Marlene.

I sipped a gin and tonic while she sucked a violent-looking cocktail through a straw. I was still dazed having received notification from the bank that the cheque for ten thousand pounds had bounced, while querying if I had mislaid any of my cards as a transaction undertaken in Cyprus looked highly irregular. I had no choice but to put everything on stop.

I contacted the airport to see if the car was there the week after Laurence had left. He had seemingly disappeared into thin air, as despite trying every conceivable way possible to contact him, I had not heard a single word. There was no sign of the car and Laurence had never boarded the plane. In the meantime his creditors were crawling out of the woodwork and some of them were turning quite nasty. I could only describe myself as shell-shocked.

Marlene finished her cocktail noisily and licking her lips nodded towards the bar.

"Remember the last time we was in 'ere and there was that geezer in the tweed jacket?" Unsurprisingly, Marlene and I did not mix in the same circles, so she had no idea, 'that geezer' had subsequently become my betrothed. I nodded.

"I went out with him once, you know. Right la-di-da type. Didn't have a bleedin' bean either. Cost me an arm and leg that night. Proper con merchant he was. Only caught me out once though, I wouldn't go out with him again. I mean, I know I'm not the sharpest knife in the drawer, but I ain't bleedin' stupid now am I?"

I had to agree.

"Your round, Marlene," I told her. "And I think I'll have one of those cocktails. It is happy hour after all."

End

Dictation

She found herself, allowing herself,
To want to trace the hollow of his throat.
She stared at the opening of his shirt,
Fresh blue slit against brown skin
And focused on the soft rise
Of flesh as he spoke.
She made a fist, holding herself in,
Not hearing words, despite
The moving pen across the page.

She noted the arrogant tilt of chin
Colouring lips she'd drawn, and watched
As he licked a slightly prominent tooth
Pushing it back between words, the
merest lisp.
And wondered how it would be
To kiss that lisp with coloured lips?

She felt her fingers fumble at her ear
And dragged her hands back to her lap,
Nodding, as he flicked the phone
Against his face. The eyes flashed grey,
With flecks of chocolate and maroon
Like stones washed upon a beach,
Made wet with sea, or surf or tears.

His fingers, slim and long and straight
Slammed shut the diary on the desk.
She jumped and fluttered to her feet.
You have all that you need, I think?
She looked directly at the sun,
Burned hot, was blinded yet again.
Yes, quite all I need, for now, she said,
As coolly as the furnace, would allow.

The Adventuress

She was home, at last. Closing the large hall door, she stood to take it all in: oak staircase, grandfather clock, Chinese rug, all as it should be, nothing changed. But in fact everything had, she knew that.

"Papa! Papa!" she called. Her name for him, a hangover from the convent. How she had loved that homely little school, where she felt safe and protected, Sister Magdalene, her favourite nun always making her feel so very special. It was she who had first called Father 'Papa'— she remembered the occasion distinctly. They had just finished a French lesson and she was eager to impress him with her few, new words.

"Véronique, is this your papa? The big car, 'e has come."

Ronnie ran to the window. The Bentley drifting into view through the summer haze, her father at the wheel, hair Brylcreemed back from his tanned face, ivory cigarette holder held in a bite between his bright, white smile. He left the car door open as he flew up the steps, taking two at a time, desperate to see his darling girl.

"Papa!" she had called as she ran to him. "I'm learning French!"

He swept her up in his broad embrace.

"Ah, ma petite, très bien." He kissed her cheek. "Ça va?"

"Ça va bien, Papa," she replied as he placed her back on terra firma. He beamed at the young nun, who watched from the shadows as father and child reunited.

"Her accent is sublime," he told her. "Your influence no doubt, Sister."

The nun blushed beneath her novice's veil.

"Merci, monsieur." And giving a short curtsey, she bade her favourite pupil farewell for the summer break.

It was the quiet French nun who had been her inspiration, filling her head with tales of missionary colleagues flung far across the globe: brave, emboldened women providing food and shelter for the poor and hungry. Sister Magdalene had showed her pictures of starving children, ravaged women, and thin, beaten men, eyes staring bemused into the camera. She had devoured everything she could about the work carried out in India's crowded cities, Africa's scorched savannahs and the parched prairies of Latin America.

Fuelled with a sense of injustice, a desire to redress the balance and right whatever wrongs she could, Ronnie announced she would become a nurse, better still a midwife and was going to work overseas, supporting the missions — it was her calling.

Her mother had been dismayed. Their beautiful, cosseted princess forsaking England's rolling shires for the heat and squalor of a foreign land. Her father was unsurprised. She had his passion, his pioneering spirit and needed to make her mark in the world. He was proud she had found her vocation but still he worried — they all worried.

Where was Sister Magdalene now, Ronnie wondered. The convent long gone, the pretty Queen Anne house and schoolrooms turned into a country retreat complete with golf course. A haven for stressed-out stockbrokers and their bored and boring wives. She, on the other hand, had become an adventuress.

"Papa!" she called out again, more loudly this time. One of her brothers had told her Father was going deaf, although she found that hard to believe. Silence. She stood watching dust mites dance as the last of the evening sun shimmered through the stained glass.

She pushed open the door to his study. He hated to be disturbed when he was working. No one sat at the desk but a curl of smoke from the ashtray gave him away. She stepped in front of the armchair, ready to throw herself onto his lap. His eyes were closed. He was sleeping — the afternoon nap he always denied. She knelt before him.

"Papa," she whispered. He would know it was she, calling through his dreams. The others called him Dad, but she liked to keep her own name for him. His eyelids flickered.

"Good grief, my African queen, am I dreaming?" He closed his eyes again, teasing.

"Papa, it's me, Ronnie." She tugged at his sleeve, the olive green corduroy he favoured at home. He lunged at her laughing, clasping her in his arms. She squealed.

"You came. I knew you would. Mother said not. It's too far. Too many sick babies need her. And here you are. Home for my birthday." He gave a small cough, eyes filled briefly with tears. "Bloody lame excuse to come back, but here you are nonetheless."

"I've missed three birthdays, thought I'd better make the big one." She gave him a serious look. "Don't want cutting out of the will, left penniless on a far-flung continent." They chuckled. A family joke. Even Harrow, the Labrador, endured this threat, giving his master a sideways glance, in case it might come to pass.

"How are you, Ron?" He lifted her chin with his big, countryman hand.

"Fighting fit!" she replied, using his quip, yet could not meet his gaze.

"I received your letter." He watched her. "Do you want to talk?"

She shook her head. "Not now, not ever really. I shouldn't have sent it."

The door flew open.

"You made it!" Her mother stood, smiling. "I told him, too far, too busy, too much to ask."

She grinned back. Mother was wearing her 'work clothes', the ubiquitous pearls lumpily hidden beneath her sweater.

"There's so much to do." She took her eldest child by the arm. "First he didn't want a party, then he changed his mind, now he's invited half the county and the other half will turn up anyway." She was laughing as they strode out. "Thank goodness I've your room ready." She gave her husband a look. "He said you'd come."

Her father sat back in his chair, waggled his fingers in a little wave as they disappeared. Now was not the time, but they would talk. He would hear her out and help as best he could, before it was too late.

Having unpacked, she went to find him in the greenhouse, he was watering the lilies. It would soon be warm enough to put the pots outside. He liked an extravagant display on the steps of the terrace, the heavy scent making its mark on rare summery nights.

The jangle of her bracelets made him look up. She appeared somehow more exotic: lights in her hair, golden skin, his soft English rose blooming into an orchid.

"I haven't asked about Geoffrey, is he busy?" He pulled a couple of dying leaves from a plant. "Away a lot, I imagine."

Geoffrey had been such a relief. They met at a cocktail party, something to do with the Foreign Office and had fallen instantly in love, the same background, same ideals, both about to embark on a great adventure; a perfect match. Geoffrey had made the whole thing more bearable, for the whole family.

"It's the nature of his work. The consulate expects so much," she said, watching her brothers through the misty glass, hauling at the tarpaulin as they worked with the men to erect the marquee.

"We haven't had a proper party since your wedding." Her father's eyes followed her gaze.

"Five years," she said, rubbing her left hand. Had he noticed her ring was missing?

"How long have you been seeing him, this other man?" her father asked, quite casually.

She turned sharply, startled at his directness.

"His name is Brody. Daniel Brody."

She needed to say his name out loud. She missed him so much she was frightened he was a figment of her imagination, like the invisible friends of her childhood, as if she had created him to fill the void, dissolve the loneliness.

"How long have you been having an affair with Mr Brody then?"

An affair. She baulked at his words. But it was true, an affair was precisely what it was. But he had missed out the word love — it was a *love* affair.

"Around eighteen months." She knew to the second; why was she trying to appear so nonchalant when every minute she spent with him was scorched through her like a brand?

"Is he married too?" he asked, recalling her letter, a brief, sad scrawl filled with pain. He had carried the ache ever since.

Was she married? She did not feel married, not to Geoffrey anyway. Besides he was married to his job.

"No, a bachelor, he runs —"

"A coffee plantation in Tanganyika, I know."

She gave a crooked smile. Of course he knew. Her father was a self-made man, powerful, protective. He would need to know what kind of man had inveigled his highly principled, very proper daughter, had her so bewitched she had broken her marriage vows and become the subject of gossip, scandalous tittle-tattle that had reached even the cloistered corridors of his club.

"And Geoffrey?" he prodded gently.

"Oh, he doesn't know, wouldn't care less anyway, he's so wrapped up in his work."

He saw a blush of anger warm her throat and was relieved she still felt something for her husband, if only rage.

Shouts and raucous laughter drifted across the lawn. One side of the marquee had fallen down and Harrow was trapped beneath the canvas. He was running wildly in circles, trying to break free.

"Poor Harrow," she cried, and flew to release him, her brothers too helpless with laughter to do anything at all.

How she adored the party; all the friends and neighbours she had not seen for so long, laughing in the sunshine. She was even pleased to see people she loathed: the beetroot-faced vicar and his stuttery wife; the leering greengrocer and his still pimply assistant; and mad Mrs Burgoyne, who they said murdered her husband and ate carrots to see in the dark as she prowled the village – Ronnie was delighted to see them all.

And then there were the children, so many children! All her friends had at least two. Even couples she could never imagine having sex had a babe apiece in their arms. Yet she, still childless, had been the first to marry, barely twenty years old, running away with Geoffrey to a new life, a fresh frontier, dreaming of their African-born children, instantly exotic, totally adored. The dream was fading.

Her father found her sitting on a step, the champagne abandoned, bubbles burst. She was looking out to the west, charcoal streaks of dusk smeared across twilight pink. Not the big, blown sky of Africa but exquisite in its own way.

"When will you go back?" he asked.

"In a week, maybe two. I've missed you all so much." She kept her tone light, but he had seen the melancholy in her eyes when she thought no one was looking, watching the children with such longing, it almost broke his heart.

"And who will you go back to, I wonder?"

She did not reply straight away, but touched the finger on her left hand. She had stopped wearing her ring, telling Geoffrey she had a splinter from chopping bamboo; he had tutted at so unwifely a task. Now Harrow had come to slide between them, the two he loved best and putting his chin on her knee, the dog gazed at her unblinkingly.

"Ronnie!" her mother called. "Come quickly, the telephone!"

She kissed Harrow on the nose and squeezing her father's shoulder, walked back to the house.

Her visit was cut short. Excellent news: Geoffrey promoted; a good position at a new station; she must return at once, to pack, move on. The receiver became a dead weight in her hands. She was suddenly weary, far too tired to contemplate cases and chaos, her head and heart disarrayed, fragmented. She was sure in moving she would leave bits of herself behind, and in doing so become less.

Her father had insisted on taking her to the airport, a tiring drive for him these days but he would not hear of a taxicab and did not trust her brothers with such precious cargo. Yet he and she had been more or less silent all the way, save for Harrow on the back seat, whining occasionally, the solemnity of the atmosphere making him miserable.

She felt tears rise when she saw the sign for the airport and there was no going back.

"Oh, Papa, it's such a mess. Why do I feel so wretched, as if I've done something wrong," she said in a quiet voice. Perhaps her brothers were right. He seemed not to hear. His handsome profile just looked straight ahead, frowning slightly against the glare of the day.

They would land soon. From the window of the aeroplane she could see Kilimanjaro's snow-covered peak and, looking out, a swathe of cloud beneath seemed like snow too, crinkled in drifts, puffed up in piles, just like the winter they thought would never end when her father had worn an old beaver coat to dig a trench through the snow to the greenhouse and covered everything in lint, for fear the interminable cold would kill his precious plants.

Oh, how she wished the world, the whole entire world, could look just like this. White and pure and all covered up in something soft and silent, so that whatever had changed was hidden. Hidden beneath the drift with everything smoothed over, like a morning in deep mid-winter when drawing back the curtains she would be blinded by bright white snow, and all would be changed, the entire landscape obliterated in the night, everything that had gone before vanished. And waking her brothers she would rush out, arms wide to embrace it, and she remembered the joy, the sheer joy of it. Such joy.

The announcement to fasten seatbelts came. She would soon have to relinquish the cool comfort of the aircraft for the heat and chaos of this wondrous land, her adopted home, where the only snow covered the unreachable top of a forbidden mountain.

Pulling herself together, she gathered her things, and reaching for her bag she noticed an envelope slid inside. She opened it. It contained a cheque for a thousand pounds made out in her father's hand, and a note.

'For the escape fund … or not. Ton coeur brisé se réparera rapidement.'

Your broken heart will soon mend.

And taking the ring from her purse, she slipped it back on her finger; it felt fine. It would have to, even though the splinter still remained.

End

Friends in Graveyards

I stopped today to visit a friend in a
graveyard,
Not grandparents, or friends of
grandparents
Or parents, or friends of parents
Or parents of friends …
A friend of mine, my friend.
And I thought. I have come to this time
then,
A time when there are friends of mine in
graveyards.
And I considered, there's a lot to look
forward to
The more friends in graveyards the better,
If you catch my meaning.
Plenty to see on the other side.
Plenty waiting to greet me.
The more the merrier, there'll be a hell of
a hooley
If you pardon the pun.
And I shall look forward to it.
It's the only way.

Moniack Mhor

Here I am in Inverness

Brought the monster

With me.

A Seed of Doubt

Thomas could see black spiked turrets poking into the pale sky as the coach passed through the vast gateway, rattling along the leafless tree-lined avenue and on towards the house.

Determined to remain unimpressed, he gripped the seat as the murmuring of his fellow travellers became gasps of delight, mounting to a crescendo of excited babble as the coach swept by the lake, swinging round to take in the full view of the magnificent gothic pile before juddering to a halt on the gravel. The east and west wings draped either side of the main house, sweeping backwards as if to formally present the glittering façade of glass and golden stone that was Moorcroft Hall.

They bustled from the coach, as smiling 'Welcomers' in polo-shirts bearing the Moorcroft Crest, ushered them up a mountain of steps and into a reception hall the size of half a football pitch. A fireplace, which could accommodate five full-grown adults standing in a row, was ablaze with a forest of logs. The gleaming floor reflected the galleried landing above and a shimmering marble staircase spilled to the ground, as a gossamer figure sailed daintily earthwards, sunbeams from the stained-glass window bursting in all directions as it sashayed towards them. Those gathered below blinked as one, speechless.

"Welcome, welcome, newest friends only just met," the sheeny, gossamer-clad figure boomed, breaking the spell as it tip-toed around their defensive semi-circle, touching each in turn, confirming that the being with the booming voice was indeed solid matter, possibly human, species or sex yet to be determined.

"I'm Willoughby, your host for what's going to be a truly memorable weekend," the now named Willoughby beamed, revealing disconcertingly brilliant teeth. "Reception drinks are being served in the morning room. You no doubt all got to know each other intimately on the bus and those with single rooms might want to double up already, who knows?"

Willoughby laughed appreciatively at his own, apparently huge joke, fox-trotting towards an open doorway with silent footsteps.

"Let's do the formal stuff first and agree our programme over a nice glass of chilled Chablis." He pronounced Chablis as *chabless* and referring to the notes on his clipboard tutted as if he realised this was not the 'Soooo Don't Want to be Single!' group he thought it was.

Thomas hung back, waiting for the last of them to pass through to the other room, and then, as quietly as the polished floor would allow, he turned on his heel, pulling the squeaky wheelie suitcase behind him.

"Ahem," a feigned cough echoed. "This way, sir. You'll be fine once you know what's what." Willoughby was standing in the doorway. Thomas half turned, unsure. "Sir, *please*, the programme is about to begin." The twirling figure in floaty layers seemingly had a core of steel.

The room beyond grew silent. He pulled the squeaky wheels back across the floor. "You must be Thomas." Willoughby shook his hand. Thomas nodded. The hand he held was ice cold.

Later, sitting on the bed in the small room one of the 'Welcomers' had made such a great fuss of showing off, even guiding him round the tiny bathroom – at one point he thought the poor chap was actually going to demonstrate how to flush the loo — Thomas sighed heavily.

He went to the only window, set high in the wall. He could just about see out but there was not much of a view. His room appeared to be in one of the hall's many turrets, the turret facing the rear of the house; if he stood on tip-toe he could make out a vegetable patch in a walled garden and, craning his neck to the right, the corner of a greenhouse. He thought he saw a man, bent over, dressed in overalls, but the light was fading and he was weary. The day had grown more grey and his view, considering the grandeur of the house and its landscape, positively gloomy. He kicked the squeaky, wheelie suitcase. Perhaps when they were all in bed he could call a taxi and go home.

He must have dozed off. There was a tapping noise, a creak and a shaft of light seared the darkness. Panic pounded in his chest. Where was he?

A lamp snapped on.

"Sorry to disturb but you didn't come down for supper. Something on a tray, will that suit?" Willoughby was hovering at the foot of the bed. Thomas could taste perspiration on his upper lip. "Just this once mind. You'll have to join in tomorrow. I know it's hard but just take that first step. It'll be worth it, you'll see."

Everything on the tray was freezing cold, even the soup, yet the ice cream had melted — a swirling splodge of raspberry in a creamy frame, like blood dripped in milk. Thomas felt his stomach lurch and pushed the tray away. He fumbled in his pocket for a sleeping pill, swallowed it down and, pulling the eiderdown over his head, stayed like that until dawn.

As soon as Thomas opened his door the following morning Willoughby appeared, wearing what looked like a translucent tracksuit.

"Ah, there you are, excellent. Breakfast and then straight into our first session, Bereavement for Beginners." He gave that awful grimace he seemed to think was a reassuring smile.

Thomas stifled a sigh and followed the glowing figure downstairs.

Sitting in the corner of the palatial former drawing room for the dreaded first session, Thomas could see across the courtyard to the edge of the walled garden. He recognised the greenhouse he had spotted from his turret window. A man with white hair appeared at the gateway, pushing an ancient wheelbarrow. The man stood up, straightened his back and smiled a big broad grin straight at Thomas and then trundled off into the distance. Thomas watched him leave with longing.

It felt like a meeting of Alcoholics Anonymous, with members of the group volunteering to stand up and recount personal experiences. Some had been tearful, choked with emotion, while others had been desperate to pass on their pain. Thomas felt nothing. He just sat there wondering if the woman conducting the session had ever lost so much as an earring, let alone a life partner. He was desperate to escape, so while the others chatted mutely over coffee, he slipped quickly away and out into the crisp March morning.

He drew a long, deep breath of air and gripping his nostrils, blew hard as if to dislodge a blockage. Sniffing, he could smell burning, as tendrils of smoke drifted a soft musky scent towards him through the gap where the gate to the walled garden stood ajar. Stealthily, he crossed the frosty stone flags, pulling the gate behind him and, leaning against it, closed his eyes. When he opened them, he could see the old gardener through the greenhouse. The man looked up, his crinkly eyes twinkled as grubby hands beckoned Thomas in.

"It's you I saw in there, staring out the window, wishing you were somewhere else?" the man said. Thomas nodded.

"What's it this time? Teach Yourself Charisma? Write a Best Seller in a Weekend? Or How to Find your Perfect Partner?" There was a smile about the man's mouth.

"Bereavement and Beyond." Thomas picked up one of the pots, nearly dropping it as the man's booming laughter ricocheted around the glass.

"Well, that's a good one! A total riot. Got to be one of the best yet. What will they think of next?" No sympathy. No word of condolence. "No wonder you look so desperate. You never know, you might discover your charisma, find your perfect partner and write a best seller about the whole bloody thing." He chortled throatily to himself, emptying the last of the earth from the pots into a large tray, sifting it through with his fingers.

"My daughter, Denise, booked it. It was her idea, she insisted I came," Thomas said dolefully.

"A bit of a bossy boots is she?" the other man asked.

"She's just worried about me. I've been a bit weird since her mother died."

The man was picking tiny lumps gently out of the soil, transferring them into individual containers then covering them tenderly with moist black peat.

"What are you doing?" Thomas asked.

"Giving 'em a second chance. Sometimes things are best left quietly in the darkness. If there's life there, it'll come back, eventually." The man rubbed his chin, giving Thomas the once over. "You're not a gardener?"

"No, my wife looked after that side of things. I work away a lot, not much time for gardening."

"Gardening doesn't take time. It's other things take time away from gardening." The old man was watching him with shrewd eyes.

A bell clanged across the courtyard. Thomas looked up.

"Better get back to your bereavement buddies. What's on the agenda this afternoon, the A to Z of embalming ?" the man grinned. Thomas shrugged. "Come back at tea time. I've got a flask'll do you more good."

"Oh, what's that then?"

"Blackcurrant vodka."

Thomas cheered a little, albeit briefly.

It was easy for Thomas to duck out at four o'clock. Willoughby had given them an 'unstructured' hour to help deal with any guilt relating to the dearly departed. The gardener was in the greenhouse, warming himself by a rusty stove. He waved Thomas in and handed him a mug of jewel-coloured liquid. Thomas sipped, as sweet nectar burned his throat, warming his chest instantly.

"Swig it back, man," the gardener insisted. "Plenty more where that came from. Good wife was she?" the gardener asked after a while.

"I thought so." Thomas took a generous refill. "Until she died anyway."

The old man signalled for him to continue. Thomas took a deep breath.

"Clearing out her things, I found stuff, letters and photographs, some old, some not so old, but all from people I didn't know."

"You mean people you didn't *know* about. Men?"

Thomas nodded.

"How many men?"

"Three or four."

"Were they graphic, these letters? Had she been intimate with these men? Were they lovers?"

"Not really clear. Nothing graphic, more flirting, talking about dinner dates, dancing, going to the movies together, that sort of thing," Thomas was surprised he was just blurting it all out. Something he had not even been able to think about, let alone talk about. Something that had been lodged in his chest, like a lump of granite.

"Didn't mean much then sounds like, just the company of the opposite sex and a bit of flattery more than anything, and you did say yourself, you work away a lot. She was probably just a bit lonely. You'll have lots more letters and pictures of happy family times together, I'd imagine." It was a statement. "What's the problem, do you feel betrayed?"

Thomas felt sure he should be uncomfortable having this highly personal conversation with a stranger, but nevertheless he answered.

"No, that's the problem. I don't feel anything, no grief, no anger, nothing," Thomas said, flatly.

The gardener poked the stove. "Guilt then?"

"For what?" Thomas was shocked. "I've never

been unfaithful."

"There's more than one way to stray. A mistress doesn't have to lie abed to take your heart or your soul. Other things can do it just as well — work, business, a hobby. Doesn't take much to leave a woman, even if you're still with her." The gardener poured more drinks.

Saved by the bell. Thomas quickly departed, glad to leave the old man to his twaddly, homespun wisdom.

After supper and before the session 'Rediscover Laughter', Thomas found himself alone in the greenhouse. The neat rows of pots stood silently awaiting the reawakening of the seeds inside. He lifted one to gaze at the surface and see if there was any sign of life and as he reached across, a fat envelope thudded to the floor.

It was his wife's collection of memorabilia, snaps and scraps of fanciful romance with other men, letters, photographs, ticket stubs. He had been carrying it around with him since he found it in the old suitcase, at the back of the wardrobe. She had always loved a romantic hero. She liked to go dancing, out for Italian meals, popcorn at the movies … she had no real hobbies to speak of, except gardening, she loved to grow flowers — roses were her favourite, corny but true.

Thomas bent to the ground and, snatching the bundle up, lifted the lid of the stove and thrust the envelope inside. Grabbing the poker he pushed the paper against the embers until it smouldered and burst into flame, devouring the words and smiling faces of memories that did not belong to him, memories and photos of a woman he had always assumed did.

"Well done, that was just going out I reckon." The old man was standing behind him. He proffered a mug of the blackcurrant vodka. Thomas, who had never been a drinker, knocked it straight back, hoping it would dissolve the granite.

The next morning, Willoughby and the 'Welcomers' were lined along the steps, shaking hands and saying sincere goodbyes to everyone.

"I hope that helped." Willoughby looked deep into Thomas's face.

"Dunno if I'm honest. I liked the old gardener though. Nice line in blackcurrant vodka."

Willoughby arched an eyebrow. "So, it was you then. I wondered who he would choose this time."

Thomas tilted his head. "Choose?"

"Oh yes, he always picks one we can't help does old Gabriel. Cost effective too. No salary to find for a counsellor from the other side. A spirit guide in more ways than one, that's what we call him." He gave

Thomas a brief hug. "I'm so pleased for you."

Thomas sat at the back of the coach, straining to catch a last glimpse of the walled garden as they drove away. He thought he could see him, Gabriel, and he was sure he waved. But maybe not.

"Did it help, Dad?" Denise was anxious. Her father had been so cold, so unfeeling since Mum died. He had hardly said a word, she really was at her wits' end.

"Nah, I hate all that new age claptrap, you know I do!" Thomas replied, putting the scissors back in the drawer. He had just finished framing an old photograph, one of himself and his wife, taken years ago. She looked pink and shiny. They had been dancing in a competition; they were quite good back in the day. He placed a rose from the garden in a champagne glass beside it. Standing back, he was pleased with his work.

"Make any friends? Decide on a new hobby?" Denise asked, hopefully.

"Might try gardening," Thomas said, giving the girl in the photograph his sunniest smile.

End

Marco – My Eldest

He does not know how old he is, could not care less,
Like a child before it's programmed to count
Candles on cake – abuse, that is!
How relevant can it be? Not at all.

You have either seen or not seen.
The newness of experience is the same,
A thrill, a spook, a scare, a pleasure or a pain.

And he will pay no heed to any 'warnings' on the tin
So gallops up the hill, mane and tail streaking in the wind,
For joy, for joy, for joy …

And at the top, a breath, a rest, to view the world, spread all around,
An emerald cloak with jewels embroidered in.
He does not own an inch of it, and yet there it lies, all his.

He takes a bite of grass. The plain earth feeds him too, a gift from God.

And snorting softly, smells the scent that is his world,
As new as on the day he strove to stand on shaking legs
And felt the comfort close of another mother, but yet the same
And so she says, come now, enough, we'll saunter home,
The evening streaked with topaz and citrine.

He calls to friends, to say I am returned.
And looks to ask if supper may be due?
She smiles and hides the 'veteran mix' away.
He doesn't know his age, but can he read?
She couldn't say.

The Messenger

The muffled laughter blew carelessly upward through the open window, carried easily on the warm summer air. I recognised the sound instantly as belonging to Peggy and with great stealth crawled silently from beneath the blanket, across the bare floor towards the casement. The curtain lace brushed my hair as I knelt, straining my ears to hear their love words and laughter.

The sentences were indistinct, but Peggy's soft, tinkling voice floated gently on the breeze and I could tell by the tone that she was nervous and excited.

I did not fully understand the meaning of the noises below the window and the calm, star-filled summer sky, but I knew with the groping awareness of adolescence that it was thrilling and I giggled to myself, squeezing my eyes shut with delight. It was the first of many such encounters that summer but the tantalising goodbyes always followed the same pattern. After many protests and more laughter, they would break off abruptly and I would hear the hall door close quietly. As her light steps ascended the stairwell, I would dive from the window to the bed in one movement, praying my heaving chest did not give me away.

She would enter the room softly, slipping out of her dress and brushing her copper curls loose. I would lift an eyelid to watch her smile in the half-light, a smile I had seen upon her lips after many laughing evenings that summer. Then she would slide noiselessly beneath the cover beside me.

I knew she did not sleep for what seemed like hours for I could feel her wakefulness and tingling excitement, yet I would grow weary for slumber, and unable to share outwardly in her joy for fear of a scolding, would soon be asleep.

"Where were you last night?" Mother would ask each morning after Peggy's excursions.

"Round at Sarah's", "Only in Dwyers", "Up at the Hall" came the standard replies, issued from cherubic lips which tightened quickly after speaking, no further information volunteered.

Mother would bang the kettle off the range in frustration and Peggy would toss her auburn head towards the window. Stalemate as usual.

Thankfully, things were considerably less tense when Father was home. Peggy smiled most of the time, especially when she looked at him.

"Don't be always at the child," I heard him chide Mother more than once, listening intently for fear the 'child' was me. It was always Peggy.

Mother would only grunt in reply and bang more pots around the kitchen. I would slither to the doorway and sometimes see him slip his arm around Mother's ample waist, kissing the ever-present twist of greying hair piled atop her head.

"Don't be worrying, woman," he would whisper, and she would frown pushing him playfully away.

I loved it when Father was home. When school and work was done, he would pull me onto his knee, letting me fill his pipe for him and light it too. Then he would talk to me, tales of the sea and faraway places, and he would cuddle me, kissing my dark, cropped hair, calling me his little 'Molly Coddle' and I would go to bed with his familiar tobacco and leather scent filling my nostrils and my dreams.

Peggy went out almost every evening but Mother did not seem to mind so much when Father was there. Anyway, he always stayed up for her no matter what the hour and he would never scold her, though there would be no giggling at the door if he was home.

The brothers were just huge, hulking giants to me then, never threatening or offensive but familiar strangers, like people you see regularly in the street yet never speak to. There were three of them: Daniel, named after Father, Christy and James. They were all years older than me, years older than Peggy even and were away often, sometimes with Father, sometimes without.

Mother cooked huge pots of stew when they were home and the loaves of bread she baked seemed endless. I used to make a sixpence or two out of boot-cleaning and was the envy of the whole street as I sucked barley sugar from one end of the week to the next and it not even Christmas.

The brothers would laugh and slap their thighs late at night around the fire in the kitchen and I would watch from the stairs, laughing with them but unaware of the joke. Mother would 'tut' and shake her head as if bemused by their antics. Then they would joke with her and make her smile until Christy swore and she beat him half-heartedly around the head, then turn and chase me up the stairs, knowing full well I was there all the time.

The joy that was with Peggy that summer faded towards the autumn and a much more intense and nerve-racked emotion grew behind the almond-shaped blue eyes.

I lay awake beside her as she sobbed through many sleepless nights and our tiny room was filled with the anguish of it all.

Once, she pulled me to her, thinking me asleep, and whispered harshly, "Oh Molly, Molly may God spare you the longing." And I felt the tears trickle slowly through my hair to my scalp.

The next time Father came home he said I was almost a woman, and indeed I was much taller and nearly twelve. Christy came with him and Peggy and I were pleased because we did not have to give up our bedroom. Christy would sleep on a mattress in the front parlour, which meant not disturbing the entire house when he came home singing or cursing. Mind, I learned some new words to share in the school yard right enough.

When the others came home the mattress went upstairs and all the men shared our room. Peggy made a bed for herself in the parlour and I had to sleep with Mother. Mother snored but would cuddle me if it was cold, unlike Peggy who never cuddled up and would scream out if I accidently lay on her hair whatever the hour.

Peggy stood for ages in front of the looking glass that night, brushing her hair and pinching her cheeks, twirling endlessly in the misty, pale peach dress that had been hanging beneath brown paper on the back of the door since her trip to Dublin.

The setting sunlight lit her face in the softening glow of evening and I thought her the most beautiful thing I had ever seen. Sighing, I told her so and she tugged my hair playfully.

"Ah, Molly, one day you'll look beautiful too, and some nice man will come calling on you and then what would Father say?"

She made no comment on the blush that grew swiftly from my throat to my face, just smiled and twirled finally before tripping lightly down the stair and out into the evening.

I must have dozed, for it wasn't love talk and laughter that woke me that night but the loud banging of the hall door and Mother's voice raised high-pitched in anger. The words were not clear, so I clambered out of bed and went to the landing, gazing down the wooden stairs towards the light from the half-open door into the kitchen.

"Now, Kathleen, there's no need for such harsh words, she's just a girl yet," Father was saying softly but firmly, as was his way.

"It's a shame and a disgrace and I'll have no more of it." Mother's voice was fretful. "You've said yourself he's a drunkard and a no-good, without even a skill on the ship and only taken on by the master because he's his nephew."

A chair scraped across the floor and Father eased his huge frame into it.

"Daddy, say it's not so," declared Peggy. "Say she's lying."

"Whist, child, your mother's no liar and the man's no good. It's best you see the back of him."

Peggy whined as if a knife had pierced her heart and Mother sighed heavily. I crawled closer so I could see Father in his chair through the door. Mother stood behind him, her brow furrowed, her night-gown pulled around her tightly.

"But Daddy, I'll make good of him, I'm not a child, I know what I'm doing. Give him a chance Daddy. You'll see a change in him, I promise you that."

Father shook his head dolefully and filled his pipe.

"I'd no idea it t'was he you were stepping out with, Margaret." I knew it was serious when he used her full name. "He's not for you, nor to take the good name of this family. I'm sorry, but there you have it."

Peggy started to cry.

"But Daddy he's asked me to marry him, honestly – so you can see he wants the best for me."

"Yes, but what of his other wife or two?" interrupted mother, blazing eyes scorching a look from one to the other.

Peggy flew to Father and threw herself at his lap, sobbing and pleading. Mother placed her hand firmly upon his shoulder and he slumped further into his chair.

"She's always having sly digs about me getting married." Peggy glanced back accusingly at Mother. "I thought she'd be pleased."

"I would be pleased if it was marriage to someone halfway decent. God knows you've made enough mistakes." Mother's voice was barely above a whisper.

"One mistake! One mistake!" Peggy shrieked back at her.

"Enough, child," Father said quietly, smoothing her copper crown with his fingertips. Peggy leapt to her feet, bright eyes filled with tears.

"I'm not a child anymore, Father and you'll have to get used to that. I'll marry Kieran Kelly whether you like it or not. And as I've often heard Mother say, there aren't many choices left to me at this stage!" And with that she stormed from the room, nearly tripping over me in her haste.

Father rose to follow but Mother held him back and for fear of being discovered I ran swiftly after Peggy, who had thrown herself sobbing onto the bed.

It was soon after that I became the go-between, running messages to and from Peggy and the tall dark stranger whose name I had first heard on that fateful night. He was indeed handsome, with features as dreamlike as the pictures I'd seen of the film star Rudolf Valentino. Although I had never been to a picture house, Monica Cassidy's elder sister kept a collection hidden in the clothes trunk under the bed.

I was tasked with carrying little notes smelling of lavender water from Peggy to his lodging rooms down by the quay. He would read them rapidly, then, smiling with white even teeth, give me an answer in an almost English accent and I would have to concentrate very hard on the words because his voice was totally captivating and I had fallen hopelessly in love with Peggy's Kieran Kelly.

I kept their illicit meetings secret, thrilled to be part of the conspiracy. Peggy had shared very little with me throughout my childhood and now that we had a secret I felt that I had finally grown-up and Peggy was my best friend as well as my sister.

The meetings went on for six weeks, with Peggy escaping at every chance. Father was convinced his beloved daughter was following his instructions and had given the blackguard the elbow but Mother was not so sure, and I overhead her telling Christy to keep an eye on Peggy of an evening. Peggy was pleased with this information and we had to cover her tracks extra carefully with Christy alerted to the situation. However,

Christy preferred the pastime of drinking stout to following his sister and pursued this with a lot more ardour, which thankfully enabled the path of true love to run more smoothly.

Father was preparing to leave again and Mother had grown more irritable when it dawned on me that Peggy's Kieran must be sailing too. The day before they left, Peggy was fraught with anxiety, hiding her emotions bravely in front of the family but confiding solemnly in me.

I was distracted with grief and broke down uncontrollably in the lane between Rourkes' lodging house and Casey's Bar, having taken the final message of rendezvous to the dashing Kieran.

Peggy made good her escape when all the house was asleep late that night and dawn had just broken when she returned. I was drowsily disturbed as she crept into bed, her usually smooth flowing hair a mane of curls and golden wildness. She was breathless and flushed and she sighed repeatedly. I nudged her in the ribs.

"Did you say goodbye, Peggy? Will Kieran be gone long? Are you not broken-hearted?"

She beckoned me to hush, and folding her arms about herself, seemed to smile with tears glistening in her eyes.

"Oh, I'll miss him Molly, for I love him dearly. But

he's mine now and he'll come home to me, he'll come home to his Peggy, I'm quite sure of that," she told me in a soft voice almost as if she were praying. Then she slept easily, the peaceful sleep of one who is quite content.

The relationship between Mother and Peggy did not improve while the men were away.

A few of the local fellows would call occasionally but they held no interest for my sister. Clerks from the corn exchange were awful bores, so Peggy said, and the dockers were so rough they made the crowd at Casey's seem like gentlemen. Even when Michael Shaunessy, formerly the man of her dreams, came home from the boys' college that summer, I had to admit that he would have an awful long way to go to take over from Kieran Kelly as the leading man in my and Peggy's fantasies.

Mother grew twitchy as Peggy's twenty-ninth birthday approached.

"Your Auntie Mary was only saying the other day that she couldn't believe you're almost that age and no sign of a wedding yet."

Peggy looked at me, then rolled her eyes up to heaven.

"I told her, you know Peggy, there's no-one in the whole town good enough for her."

"True enough, there's no-one round here I'd marry off to a dog, that's for sure," said Peggy haughtily.

"I wouldn't have thought you could afford to be so choosey my girl!" sniped Mother, her eyes darting quickly from Peggy to me and back.

"I've made my choice," came the hissed reply, as she banged down the cup she was drying and marched through the back door.

The question of my elder sister's marital status always seemed to arise rather pointedly around the time of her birthday. It was true, all the girls of Peggy's age were married and had at least one child, save for Francie Keogh who went to be a nun and came back after just two years. But, sadly for Francie, so far her romantic encounters were proving to be as successful as her religious ones.

I sided totally with Peggy, not entirely sure of the facts. I knew she was easily the prettiest girl in the town, and if she chose to take her time making a match, it seemed perfectly acceptable to me. To my way of thinking, Mother should have been delighted Peggy didn't take up with the first man who came along and anyway, if Mother knew Kieran Kelly as well as I did, she'd understand why Peggy didn't want anyone else – he was well worth waiting for.

Three months passed before we got word that the men were coming home again. Mother started to scrub and clean the house in preparation and I helped her as best I could. Peggy made new curtains for the parlour and the kitchen but she wouldn't scrub the stairwell or the scullery stone floor for fear the soap would blister her skin. Yet she smiled to herself despite the scowling looks Mother gave her and I knew Kieran was returning and grew slightly ashamed of the deep joy I felt growing within me.

Again the meeting was in secret and with all the excitement of Father's return with Daniel, James and Christy, Mother didn't comment too harshly on Peggy's swift departure after dinner. I knew that she was making her way down to the chapel grounds as fast as her cornflower blue slippers would take her, for that was where they had met on the final evening of his leave.

I had cunningly left the evening free myself, explaining to Monica, my best pal, that I would have to stay home with Daddy. She understood. Her father was on the boat too but she didn't care for him too much — he smelled of rum and sometimes, if she didn't get out of the way quickly enough, he'd give her a clatter on the head, mistaking her for one of her brothers.

I escaped through the back door and raced towards

the chapel grounds, taking a short cut through Morgan Morrissey's timber yard, making sure I got there well ahead of Peggy.

I crouched down, running along by the wall, popping my head up at intervals until I spotted the tall, dark figure leaning against the side of the grotto, puffing irreverently on a cigarette.

He turned casually to face the gateway and I leapt over the wall, half-crawling to nestle behind a huge marble headstone bearing the inscription …*In memory of my beloved husband, lost at* … I didn't read any further as I heard the creaking of the gate and Peggy's voice calling the name of her sea-faring lover.

I edged deftly to the corner of the headstone, just in time to see him envelope her in his arms and kiss her lips hungrily. I gasped, then rammed my hand over my mouth, shocked to witness such blatant passion. I bit my lip and felt my temples throbbing with illicit excitement. I looked again and Peggy was pressed against his chest. He stroked her hair and whispered into it.

They talked for a few minutes — I couldn't hear the words — then something was said and Peggy pulled away from him sharply. I strained in vain to listen but I could clearly see her eyes widen as she looked up at him and then he moved forward across the grass with hands outstretched in pleading.

She turned her back and he swung her round roughly. I stood up from my hiding place, unconcerned about being caught. He gripped her arms tightly and she shouted for him to let her go, her eyes filled with tears, and I was torn between running to help her or running away.

Suddenly he released her and strode off in the opposite direction, towards me and the marble monument. I knelt behind the headstone again and heard Peggy's footsteps as she ran after him. His tone was angry and he said distinctly,

"Away with you woman, you're no good and everyone knows it, a fine wife you'd make."

"It's yours, it's yours," she shrieked, so distracted with anguish she did not care who heard her, though thank goodness the chapel yard was deserted.

"I'm not the first, nor the last I shouldn't wonder. You'll not make an eejit out of me and I'll not make you my wife and you know why, the evidence speaks for itself!" he bit scornfully back over his shoulder. I heard the rustle of leaves underfoot as if there was a skirmish, and then boots scrunched against the gravel as he marched off towards town.

I was horrified. What could have happened? What had been said? How could such soulful lovers be torn apart with words of hate? My mind was a mass of questions as I clawed my way blindly to the top of the headstone. I was dumbfounded. Peggy lay against the trunk of a huge chestnut tree. She looked like a paper bag someone had screwed up and thrown away, her head bent to her chest, her knees buckled under her, and with great heaving sobs she began to cry.

I dare not move. Pain swept over me like a sudden sickness and I could feel her torture but nothing on earth could make me go and comfort her.

After what seemed like hours, she wiped her face with her handkerchief and smoothed the deep blue dress she had spent hours sewing. Tossing back her proud flame-coloured head, she drew herself up and, walking a little shakily but with grim determination, she let herself through the creaking gate and strode out towards home.

I never let on I'd seen or heard the exchange between Peggy and Kieran Kelly that autumn evening in the chapel yard but Father commented on her pale, drawn face and unsmiling lips and Mother's mouth tightened into a thin white line every time she saw the tell-tale signs of red-rimmed eyes.

One evening about a week after the fateful meeting, Peggy and Father went for a long walk. Mother had been washing and ironing my clothes with strict instructions for me not to wear them and so I wasn't overly surprised when they returned and Mother told me I was going to Auntie Mary's for a while, and I sulked because Auntie Mary's bedrooms smelled of unemptied chamber pots and she made the whole house kneel to say the rosary twice a day at least.

To discover, upon my return, that Peggy's marriage to Kieran Kelly was imminent didn't come as any great shock. I assumed the lovers had been reunited and Mother, on meeting him had obviously been as captivated by the man as I.

As to the wedding arrangements, I had no idea they were hurried. We had never had a wedding before. In fact, I had never been to one officially, though I had stood outside the church when Monica's big sister Beatrice had married the year before last and Monica was a flower girl and tripped over her dress.

I asked Mother if I was to be a flower girl for Peggy and she stopped her sweeping abruptly; she seemed overcome for a moment.

"Tis only a small wedding Molly, there'll not be much fuss." She looked at me then with a rare tenderness. "I'll get you some nice flowers to carry and you can wear your new pink dress."

I was thrilled and rushed to tell Monica, who acted unimpressed, but I felt full sure she was green with envy. Not least because she too considered Kieran Kelly the living image of Valentino and there was a distinct possibility I'd get a kiss and a sixpence off my new brother-in-law. It's hard not to swagger when you have so much in prospect.

Peggy wore her peach gown from Dublin and twisted orange blossom through her hair, placing a lace veil over her head for inside the church. Mother gave her a pearl clip, which Peggy said belonged to Grandmother as I pinned it to her lace collar with great care, and then she kissed me, her face aglow with love and pride.

The small chapel was cool and quiet as Mother hustled me up the aisle and into the front pew. I kneeled in prayer, waiting for the bride to arrive, but my attention was drawn to the tall, dark figure standing uneasily across the aisle beside my brother Christy. I was taken aback. My hero looked only a pale shadow of his former self, his face drawn with dark rings of bruises around his eyes, and he slouched almost apologetically at my brother's side.

I looked up at Mother whose lids were closed, lips moving noiselessly in prayer, I looked back to Kieran and realised he must be ill. My heart went out to him and it all fell into place. That evening in the chapel yard he had tried to put Peggy off the wedding because of his obvious bad health.

A lump came to my throat — my dear, sweet, handsome idol, to love her so much. I choked back the tears and gazed in mute admiration as Peggy floated down the aisle on Father's arm. So she had decided to wed him after all — surely she was the most perfect creature in the entire world and he the most divine.

There were bottles of stout, a large boiled ham and roasted chicken on the carefully laid table in the parlour with a large bowl of steaming potatoes and a basin of freshly churned butter alongside. Auntie Mary had baked a cake which took pride of place and there was even a miniature bride and groom on the top, although the groom had an arm missing, but no one seemed to notice. It was a handsome feast.

The men crowded in first, with loud voices and raucous laughter making for the food and drink without preliminaries as was their wont. Monica stood at the back door to see Peggy and my new dress and Mother called her in so we could sit and eat cake on the stairs together. Auntie Mary and Mother were drinking what looked like water from china cups but it smelt strange and when they weren't looking Monica dipped her finger in and splashed it behind her ears like Beatrice had told her they did in the films.

I slept with Mother that night, Father and the brothers had the front parlour and Peggy went with Kieran to our room where Mother had put fresh sheets on the bed and given them her own heavy eiderdown.

This arrangement continued until it was time for the men to sail again, and Peggy grew more silent and miserable as the departure grew close. I was not that upset. She had not confided in me at all since she had married Kieran and I missed the sweet smell of her hair on the pillow now that I was with Mother. I couldn't understand why she was so obviously broken-hearted at Kieran going. He spent half his time in Casey's Bar and the other half talking to sailors and such on the quay, so it wasn't as if we saw that much of him.

Handsome as he was, he had gone down some in my estimation since the wedding. He was sullen and rather moody and spoke little to Father and the brothers. Though I tried to put his bad humour down to his illness, he was looking much better lately and his pallor was well gone. Oddly enough, Mother took to him and he often shared a joke with her when they thought no-one could hear; that was the only time he laughed in our house and Peggy laughed even less.

Monica, who thought herself well up on the subject, told me that this was not unusual. Beatrice's husband,

Michael, had been a grand chap before they wed. He had even brought Monica wine gums on one hallowed occasion, but since the wedding he hardly spoke but to say, "Yes, Beatrice" or "No, Beatrice". And now they had children, Monica said he doesn't speak at all but 'babby-talk' to the little ones.

Mother, Auntie Mary and Mrs Brady, the mid-wife, were all clambering about upstairs the night Daniel was born. I boiled pots of water on the stove in the kitchen and while they were heating ripped two old sheets into even squares as Mrs Brady had shown me. I squirmed in horror as they turned into bloodied rags outside the bedroom door at frighteningly regular intervals.

I don't know who screamed louder, Peggy or the child, but soon after Auntie Mary came trundling down the stairs grinning widely.

"It's all right, Molly me darling. She's fine and the baby is a bruiser of a fella. Now, where's the bottle? We could all do with a drop."

After discovering sometime before, that the reason for Peggy's swelling stomach was a child, I bowed to Monica's superior knowledge that once you got married and slept in the same bed as your husband, you had babies. She said everyone followed the same pattern. Yet, as one of our neighbours, Noleen Duffy had been married for two years and had no children, we could only assume that the Duffy's could afford separate beds.

I knew the baby was to be called Daniel, because the last time Father came home Peggy told him she would give a boy his name. She had seemed happy enough while she was carrying, save for that short time when Father was home and I went to sleep with her again and she cried fitfully every night, murmuring words I couldn't understand. I felt sure it was something to do with the fact that Kieran had taken on another passage and chosen not to return with Father. Though she said to Mother she was pleased he had, as they needed the money for their own place.

Baby Daniel was big and bonny and dark like his father and I loved him dearly as soon as I laid eyes on him. Peggy worshipped him and watched him every waking moment with her eyes full of pride and self-satisfaction. Though she didn't let herself go like some of the women with babies; she still did her hair and wore pretty dresses, avoiding scrubbing like the plague in case her hands reddened.

She allowed me to mind and change Daniel and even bathe him once but she would let Mother nowhere near him and if she showed any sign of love or affection Peggy would snatch him away, almost snarling.

"This child is mine, Mother, and I'll keep it that way."

Daniel was three months old when Kieran returned, tanned and smiling, bearing gifts of lace and sweet-smelling bottles.

Peggy was ecstatic, throwing her arms around him and kissing his face. He ruffled my hair, kissed mother's hand and we were both charmed and enraptured, delighted to have him home and a man about the place for a while.

He played with Daniel and presented him with a glossy white sailing ship he was too young to appreciate, but Kieran didn't seem to notice.

We moved beds again and I was delighted to discover that Daniel could share a bed with me. I cuddled him and kissed his curly head all night as he slumbered easily in my arms, contented that I would soon have another little one to cherish as Peggy and Kieran were surely sharing the same bed.

Mother hated anyone oversleeping in the morning, particularly on a Sunday, and needed little reason to screech mercilessly up the stairs at Peggy still in bed. After sometime she charged up heavily, furious because Father was home and we weren't all up to go to Mass with him. I followed. I hadn't heard Peggy stir at all and feared she was ill.

"Child, what ails you?" she whispered, fear scorching from her eyes, searching Peggy's white and swollen face.

Peggy twisted in pain in the bed and beads of perspiration sprayed from her forehead. I moved closer and Mother turned at the creaking of the floorboard. She summoned me to find Father, who after muffled consultation and much soothing of Peggy, summoned me to fetch Doctor O'Dowd, who arrived with a shiny leather bag and closed the bedroom door firmly in my face.

Sometime later, Father emerged from the room, ashen and tight-lipped. He barely glanced at me beside the door, but I noticed his eyes were ablaze with fury, an emotion not easily aroused in him.

He called Christy and James, who were standing outside the hall door enjoying a pre-Mass smoke, and after hushed words and vague exclamations they went to the kitchen and started gathering their belongings.

Mother told me to take Daniel to Auntie Mary's and stay there until she sent word for me. It was Monica who told me Peggy had been taken away in the doctor's big black car. She had seen it all from her mother's bedroom window.

"It's not another baby is it?" I asked my worldly wise companion.

"Very likely, but they've taken her to Dublin, I heard your mammy telling mine, so the child will be a 'Jackeen' and there's no mistake."

I was suitably impressed; a 'Jackeen' was almost a

foreigner. Now that would certainly up my status at the Children of Mary meetings, where even a fly caught in candlewax was deemed exciting.

Much later that evening, Mother was sitting slumped at Auntie Mary's table as my aunt poured some golden-amber liquid into a glass and, placing the glass in mother's hand, helped her raise it to her lips. She took a small sip and then the worn, tired face began to crumble and tears spilled from her pale, aching eyes.

Auntie Mary patted Mother's shoulder as I stood transfixed in the doorway. I had never seen my mother look so weary, and for her to shed a tear was beyond poleaxing.

"Oh, Mary, what have I done to deserve this cross? The girl is at death's door. There'll be two orphans I'm too old to care for and a deceased drunkard I should never have let her marry. God help us, is there no end to it?" She sobbed bitterly and Auntie Mary, catching my eye, motioned for me to take the slumbering Daniel into the other room.

I did as instructed, but in a trance, numbed by my mother's words. It was obvious now Peggy had been taken away because she was ill, indeed she was dying. I gazed down at Daniel's sleeping face, totally unaware of the turmoil about him. I clenched my fists, fighting back the tears, but it did no good. They fell hot and wet, splashing gently onto the little babe's forehead, so deep in slumber he did not stir.

When Father returned from Dublin over a week later, he said Peggy was still very ill but not going to die after all. Mother cried out with relief, mouthing a silent prayer of thanks and Father put his arms around me, half-smiling at Daniel playing at the hearth.

"How's the child, Daddy?" I asked, concerned.

"What child, love?" he said, looking quizzically at me, then Mother.

"Peggy's other child?" I said.

"There is no other child," he replied, with steel in his voice.

My heart plummeted to the floor, my dreams of another baby in shreds. The child had died, wasn't it obvious, and Father was trying to spare me the pain by pretending there was no child at all. I squeezed his hand in understanding, and holding my head high, walked out into the evening air. I would bear my grief in silence for my parents' sake. Peggy was getting better, there was joy in that; we couldn't ask God for too many miracles, I supposed.

When Peggy came home from the hospital in Dublin, she looked pale and delicate. Her rose-gold hair had faded to a shade of straw and the dark lines beneath her eyes were entrenched. Though she still looked wonderful to me yet hugging her tightly, I could feel her bones through her thin cotton gown and she smiled softly, speaking my name in a quiet, husky voice.

She lay on the settee in the parlour for many weeks after her return and though I still fed and bathed Daniel, he grew to love her again and laughed every time he saw her.

Peggy had just begun going out for short walks when the letter from the boat company came.

Mother opened it with trembling hands, but as she couldn't read very well, she handed it to me, wide-eyed and frightened. I scanned the pages quickly and a mixture of relief and sadness swept over me.

"It's not Daddy or the brothers," I said quickly to her and turned to Peggy. "It's Kieran."

Peggy's hands whitened as she gripped the side of the chair.

"It says there was a fight in San Francisco, America, and Kieran died of knife wounds two days later. They'll send his pay with Christy and some extra for the widow. That's it."

I handed the letter to Peggy, who read it slowly with wide dry eyes staring at the paper and then me in disbelief.

Mother, fearing for her health, watched her closely over the next few weeks, but Peggy seemed to take it all in her stride, getting stronger day by day and taking Daniel more and more to herself.

After a couple of months, Christy returned with Father and gave Peggy a brown package with Kieran's belongings and some paper money which she locked away in her old jewel-box, now containing the discarded wedding band.

It wasn't too long before John Byrne, a tall and rather awkward man from a small village outside Mullingar, began to call to the house. He had been a friend of Christy's for some time, though he did not seem to have my brother's drinking or gambling ways and it was obvious to all that he had eyes for my sister.

He talked for hours to Peggy, often sitting in the parlour together while I got Daniel ready for bed. He lent her books and magazines and though his face reminded me of a wrinkle-skinned, sad-eyed dog, Mother said he was nice enough, if a bit earnest and had a steady job at the post office, which was a career for life. Peggy just shrugged, unimpressed, yet continued to see him on a regular basis, though it was fair to say only John Byrne came calling these days. They rarely went out together though, and she didn't bother to do her hair or wear her pretty dresses like she used to.

It was only six months after the news of Kieran's death that Peggy left for Dublin with John Byrne, the man from the post office and my beloved Daniel. I came home from school one day and they had gone, no warning, no farewell.

Mother shook her head and carried on as normal, shuffling around the house, cooking, cleaning, sighing but a light died in Father's eyes and I couldn't make out whether it was the loss of Peggy or his sea-faring life or both, he being too old to sail by this time.

The years passed quickly and soon I was grown and the name of Kieran Kelly was never mentioned in the house again. I'd visited Peggy only once since she had left with John Byrne and Daniel, travelling all the way to Dublin by myself on the train. But my short visit there was enough and the city had weaved its exciting, breathless spell and I returned home bewitched and started saving my wages from the fish factory to enable me to go and work there. Maybe I could even secure a position in a shop; the whole idea was almost too thrilling to contemplate.

I wrote to Peggy of my intention to come to Dublin, but when she answered with a brief note after many weeks there was no mention of my great and glorious plan and certainly no invitation to stay with her until I had settled myself. This hurt me more than I cared to admit.

I was still working in the fish factory when Mother died. She had taken to her bed crippled with arthritis but Father said it was her worn out, broken old heart that had finally given up on her and that God was merciful and at least she had died in her own bed, and how even a king could only ask that much. I supposed the news that Peggy had given birth to another child and she and John Byrne were still not joined in matrimony hadn't helped her ailing spirit. I didn't say this to Father, of course, but Monica nodded in understanding when I explained the whole, sorry situation to her.

Father followed Mother to the grave in just a few short months. His funeral was desperate altogether. I just stood there beside Auntie Mary in the shadows, numbed to silence as Father Mulvany mumbled prayers and splashed holy water on the flimsy wooden coffin. Peggy hadn't arrived for either of our parents' funerals and though I wasn't surprised she didn't show up for our mother's, I had always been convinced that like me, she adored our father and would have felt bound to come and pay her last respects.

My brothers James and Daniel were still away sailing the seven seas, but Christy had found his land-legs and a bride to go with them, and when they moved into the old family home, I realised I'd be better off making the break now, and the Dublin of my dreams, though somewhat dimmed by my year of nursing Mother, still awaited my arrival.

Before I left I decided to sort through Mother's old sea-chest of papers and paraphernalia. Being a woman of few letters, she had a hallowed regard for all things written and so kept every scrap of paper that ever came into the house.

I fumbled aimlessly through the yellowing manuscripts until I found a carefully stacked bundle tied with a faded, rose-coloured braid. I lifted the package out of the box and, deciphering the traditional Celtic flourish of the Gaelic, discovered that these were the birth certificates of the entire family. Considering, quite wisely, that I would probably need mine at some later date – who knew how officious things might be in the big city — I pulled the parchment marked with my name free of the braid.

I had never seen my birth certificate before, so I gazed enthralled at the glorious script marking me officially a member of the human race then read it quickly with bemused pride. It wasn't until the second or third reading that the full implications of the details, irrefutable in black and white, began to sink into my suddenly panicking and questioning brain. There in the space marked for my mother's name were the words Margaret Kathleen Murphy. They had surely made a mistake. Margaret was Peggy's name, Mother was

Kathleen. They had mixed the names up. But where the name of my revered and adored father should have been was nothing, a blank, yellowing space filled to bursting with the most painful and terrifying void of nothingness I had ever seen.

I began to reel, as if I had been struck an almighty blow about the head and still in this dazed and agonising state, words, sentences and situations from my childhood began to rush back at me, washing me, drowning me in waves of nostalgia and realisation. Peggy was my mother, of course. All things considered now, it made perfect sense.

It explained her relationship with Mother and the hurried wedding, arranged when it was discovered she was pregnant again, this time by Kieran Kelly.

Everything fell into place. Her obsessive possession of baby Daniel, the fact that my grandmother had brought me up as her own child, and Father, dear Father, how he had tried to be fair and loving to all concerned despite how much his heart must have been breaking. And yet, he wasn't my father. I didn't have a father; Peggy had obviously refused to name him. Perhaps she didn't even know herself. Perhaps she had been forced by a stranger. It was all so dreadful, I just couldn't believe it.

I threw the piece of paper from me, hoping it would disintegrate magically into dust and the draught from the open window would blow it away, away into the dim and distant past where it belonged. I fell to my knees, a huge weight lashed to my shoulders, as the great, choking lump in my throat burst into uncontrollable sobs and hot, bitter tears spilled from my eyes, wetting the papers strewn about me.

The notion that my father wasn't my beloved father at all seemed to me the most devastating fact of the entire issue. I was desolate. I had been lied to and felt I'd been secretly despised for my entire life.

I thought long and hard about Peggy and the events leading up to and after her marriage to Kieran Kelly as I cleaned and collected my meagre belongings. Keeping my emotions in check, I decided I needed some sort of explanation before I left once and for all to take the train to the city.

Christy had taken up a position at Morgan Morrissey's timber yard and I thought that would be the best place to tackle him and say my goodbyes. I liked his wife well enough but felt that whatever was going to be said, would best be spoken out of her hearing. She had just taken Christy on and I was sure she wouldn't relish adopting the entire closet of family skeletons at the same time.

I dropped the bulging carpet bag by the yard door and was lucky enough to find my brother – my uncle —

taking a break from his labour and supping a jar of steaming tea. He seemed surprised to see me but his lifted eyebrows soon crushed across his brow when I told him I had found my birth certificate in Mother's old sea-chest.

He went to speak, but I raised my hand to still him, seating myself, careful not to damage my second-best tweed skirt, on the well-worn workbench.

"I just want to be sure, Christy. Kieran Kelly wasn't my father, was he?"

Christy blinked at the calm and candour of the question, his eyes quickly scouring the yard for fear one of his workmates might hear the shame of our family history discussed in such a frank and open way.

"Not at all," he said quietly, and then seeing my shoulders drop in disappointment at this, a sadness came over him. "He was a no-good Molly. You should be glad he wasn't your father. Sure, he came home and gave Peggy an awful pox, even after they were married and had the child. She nearly died from it."

"I know," I said, remembering her frail, fractured body as she stood in the doorway the day she returned from hospital. "Did you and the brothers follow him to America?"

Christy nodded, his eyes downcast. He knew Kieran Kelly's death had been the crippling blow to his sister's already crushed and fading spirit.

"James got into a fight with him, though Kieran was the first to pull the knife, I swear it." Fury at the memory flashed instantly across his eyes.

I didn't really want to know which of them had taken the life of their sister's husband. Even if Kieran did draw his knife first, he must have known he was a dead man when he heard the Murphy brothers were looking for him.

I sighed and stood up, checking the time against the huge brass clock at Ryan's the Ironmongers, plainly visible over the timber yard wall.

"I'll have to go now, Christy. I'm catching the train to Dublin," I announced.

He looked into my eyes.

"Is it Peggy you're going to see — about her being your mother and all?"

I shook my head with resolve. I had every reason to be bitter, seek Peggy out and confront her with my newfound knowledge, make her explain why I had been so thoroughly deceived by my entire family. And to make her realise that now, because of them, here I was left alone in a world where my true history instantly denigrated me to a pitiful and shame-filled wretch, forever having to apologise for events in which I played no part.

But I felt no anger, only a deep, dank sadness for myself and for all of us really. I wanted no part of

Peggy. She had suffered enough, and on my last visit I had found only a grey and hollow husk of the gay and beautiful young woman she once was. No, I was going to Dublin to make my own way in the future. I'd had enough of the past and the doubts and pointless secrecy it had held.

I kissed Christy briefly and collected my bag at the gate. Once I had purchased my one-way ticket and boarded the train, I settled back in my seat, rummaging in the pocket of my coat for the piece of paper which had brought the dead and soulless past back to life.

As soon as the train gained momentum and I was quite sure no other passengers were going to share my carriage, I pulled the fusty piece of parchment from my pocket. Reading its scrawling black ink for the last time, I tore it slowly and deliberately into tiny, incomprehensible pieces. Then crushing the fragments in my hand, I stood on tip-toe to open the window. A fresh rush of steam and air blasted my face, and taking a deep breath, I threw the contents of my palm out into the wind and early evening drizzle.

Suddenly overcome with relief, I returned to my seat, finding it surprisingly easy to smile at a passing railway worker who tipped his cap in my direction as we trundled purposefully by. My decision had been the right one, I concluded, biting into my soda bread supper with relish. My beginnings and the shame that went with it were not mine. It belonged to others, not to me, and from now on I felt sure I'd be better off without them or their ghosts of pity.

I sat back, the smallest tingle of excitement beginning in the very pit of my stomach, as the city loomed large and inviting before me.

End

Pandora's Box

I have a friend with whom I laugh
And yet would welcome in my bath.
A friend with whom I talk and trust,
A friend I could devour with lust.
My fingers reach to touch his hair,
I clench them back, I wouldn't dare.
His easy smile ignites my day.
He stings my eyes. I look away.

He takes my hand in friendliness,
And I am mute, I can't confess
This longing that is deep within,
My secret festers like a sin.
He doesn't know. He cannot tell.
His nearness sears my skin like hell.

He's innocent and free of blame,
My acting skills would bring me fame.
He takes no part, although he stars
In fantasies, in beds and bars.
I can't reveal the anguished pain
Of yearning I might sleep again,
To hold him as the night descends
And in the darkness, more than friends.

But passion for my friend must be
A secret kept twixt thee and me,
So stitch these lips and seal with glue,
You see, his wife's my best friend too.

Fur Coat & No Knickers

I'd never been particularly fond of Celia. She was bossy, belligerent and at times solidly boring, so I was more than taken aback when one of our circle, Lucinda I seem to recall, described me as her best friend, at her funeral of all things and I remember feeling suddenly desperately sorry for her, Celia I mean. Imagine having a best friend who didn't really like you?

Rather a raw deal I considered, and sometimes I think Celia had a raw deal in many ways. But let me rewind a bit, to when I first became vaguely aware that there might be the teeniest bit of a problem …

I was in the garden. I loathe gardening. That's not to say I dislike gardens. I adore gardens but I don't like soil under my fingernails. I always forget to clean it out, and we'd had gardeners when I was little, a whole team of them. So the nearest I came to soil was scraping vegetables and only then when cook was away and I felt inclined to make my much lauded potato salad.

I remember Celia saying, after she'd returned from her Swiss finishing school — one of the few girls of my generation to actually attend one — you couldn't have potato salad as a signature dish. It wasn't proper cooking, and besides, it was Russian salad anyway and how could I have a signature dish I didn't even know the name of? Of course, by then she had qualified as a chef, which made having any meal with her even more unbearable. She'd always been a terrifying hostess, insisting on the stuffiest of formality at her grand dinners and instructing staff to dole out the most miserly portions of concoctions I quite frankly, wouldn't give to the terriers. I used to try to make up excuses not to go but then I'd feel guilty and turn up, much to her chagrin, as it always messed up her excruciatingly precise table plan. Sometimes you just couldn't win with Celia.

Anyway, where was I? Oh yes, in the garden. She came sweeping along the path in one of her many tweedy ensembles and some sort of Gainsborough hat, exclaiming loudly in that strangled squawk she used when she disapproved.

"You cannot be *serious,* Daphne. What are they? Begonias? Petunias? Busy bloody Lizzies? Pull 'em up, pull 'em up, I tell you. Never seen such a frightful, garish mess!"

I stood back to admire the border I'd spent all morning weeding.

"I think they're rather jolly," I offered defensively, keeping hold of my fork. She could be prone to bursts of demonstrative activity, but I needn't have worried, she was far too smartly turned out on this particular occasion to fall to her knees and start uprooting my voracious display. Though I wouldn't have put it past her if she'd been in cords and one of her more elderly cashmere cardigans.

Sighing in that exasperated way she had, she went striding off towards the orangery, tutting loudly as she approached the roses.

"You really should at least try to cultivate varieties in keeping with the house, you know. It *is* early Tudor after all."

Celia had always been a bit of a brain box: loved history; knew masses about the house, as well as the baronial pile in Scotland and the title. I've never been that interested, I'm afraid, and Charles used it far more than I — the Scottish estate and the title — he said it made a huge difference, particularly when dealing with colonials, whatever that meant.

Celia often said she wished she were a baroness instead of just a plain old double-barrelled honourable, and that Barrington-Smythe wasn't that old either. But you could never call Celia plain and sadly, now we'll never call her old.

I trotted after her, hoping it was only a fleeting visit. I had planned an afternoon on the lounger in the summer house with the latest Jackie Collins, of which Celia would no doubt disapprove, just because she wouldn't consider it educational — a matter of personal opinion I have to say.

I caught up with her. She was shaking her head at a large bush laden with fragrant blooms.

"Hybrids," she spat, as if it were a swear word.

"Charles likes roses," I'd countered. "All varieties."

"Charles is a man, Daphne. A rose is the only flower men recognise, that's why they say it's their favourite. Haven't a bloody clue."

I ignored the jibe. Charles and Celia had never got on. Well, that's not entirely true. They must have liked each other once but that was a very long time ago. They were in the same circle when I was introduced to Charles. He had been working abroad — Dubai, I think — and she had been out there helping a sheik with his horses or some such. Anyway, they seemed rather matey in the early days and I wasn't that bothered about either of them, either way. I was quite a bit younger than them and still thought boys were either brash or boring. Celia had always been around, our mothers having been distant cousins, and Charles, dear Lucinda's older brother, seemed to sort of hover in the background.

Then, not long after my twenty-first birthday, he set his cap at me – as the saying goes — rather fiercely, if I remember rightly. Turning up at odd hours all over the place, sending me gifts, inviting me to this and that, wooing everyone and everything around me. So much so, Mother said I'd better marry him or she'd run away with him herself, and Father laughed, saying he would have to come too, as he was so used to having them both around all the time. It was such a happy time and I must say I did enjoy all of Charles's lovely attention. He seemed so determined that I had no choice but to fall for him in the end.

That summer was warm and sunny and very social, and Celia and I had grown a little closer because she too seemed rather fond of Charles. But when I told her we were marrying, she just gave me a withering look and left the room — left the party we were at too, I seem to remember.

I did fleetingly wonder if there had been more to it and she thought Charles more her type and whether she had hopes in that department, which I, unknowingly, had dashed. I asked Lucinda if Charles had many girlfriends before me, being twelve years my senior, and threw a few names into the hat, including Celia.

Lucinda had laughed, saying he'd been too busy carving out a career in the city, and besides, Celia had been flighty in her younger days, a real heart-breaker, with men desperate to go to bed with her, so not really what Charles was looking for at all.

Well, she certainly wasn't flighty anymore; she came across as rather bitter where men were concerned, and Charles in particular, it seemed to me. But Lucinda said Celia hated everybody's husband, and what a shame it was she didn't have one of her own to hate quietly in private like any proper wife. Lucinda could be a real card when she had a few!

Anyway, Celia couldn't make the wedding. I remember Lucinda saying she was ill or had an operation or something and was out of the country. When I told Charles he seemed disappointed and told me to send flowers to her wherever she was, and I probably did, or asked someone else to, but with everything going on I didn't give it much thought, if I'm honest. A few of the royals were coming to the wedding, and although I know they're not remotely bothered about sparkly chandeliers or shiny silver, everyone else seemed to think they were, so it was all a pretty time-consuming sort of a palaver and we didn't see her for ages after that. When we did, she seemed to have gone off men altogether, so I never mentioned the wedding, the flowers or her illness, just to be on the safe side.

Anyway, henceforth Celia and Charles had barely managed to maintain a thin veneer of civility for more than twenty years. He always made an excuse and left whichever room she entered within minutes of her arrival, and she, who could talk for England if the mood took her, rarely said more than two words to him. She did like to glare at him though, though Celia liked to glare at lots of people really.

Despite not liking men, Celia exuded an old-fashioned glamour some men found enticing and having had a few gins she told me once she missed sex. I gathered by this admission she had got close enough to one or two in her youth but beyond that I didn't like to ask. It seemed far too intimate a subject to discuss with her — heaven knows I would never have said the right thing. Though commenting on her allure as I tried to bundle my frizz into a sleek Celia-like chignon before a ball, Charles remarked she was dangerous, shutting up like a clam when I asked what he meant and then leaving the room in a hurry, saying we were late. Celia dangerous? She might have accidently waved a gun at him at a shoot or some such but, really, dangerous? Charles could be over-critical sometimes.

I often wished she and Charles made more of an effort though. It was odd because they had similar interests: horses; sailing; archaeology. In fact, they both loved digging about in deserts or battening down the hatches off some distant shore. Me, I hate the heat, am seasick in the bath and have always been allergic to horses, but there you are. They say you can't choose your family, and as I am an only child, sometimes I was rather pleased to see her, even if it did make Charles go off in a huff. But Celia had always been in my life and a shared history does become more important as one grows older, I think you'll find.

Anyway, this particular day I offered her tea but she refused.

"I said I'd like a drink, not that I was thirsty," she told me, always one of her favourite quips.

We were sitting on the terrace with a gin and tonic apiece when I noticed the emerald, that huge, almost obscene, exquisite jewel, was missing. She lifted the glass to her mouth and drained it. I'd hardly touched mine and was just about to ask where it was, when she took herself off for a refill.

I considered the missing gem. Rumour had it that Celia had been given it by an admirer and although in love, they could not marry — something about her family not being suitable and in all the time I had known her, she had never, ever, taken it off. It certainly wouldn't be at *Garrards the Jewellers* for cleaning because the ring, along with her grandmother's fabulous collection, went there precisely fourteen days before Christmas to be returned in time for our winter ball.

"Is this all you have?" she called from the kitchen. I knew she was complaining about the gin or tonic, or both.

"You didn't mind when you didn't notice it wasn't Tanqueray." I made light of it.

"Nonsense," she snapped back. "Why on earth do you think I came in to check? Filthy muck," she said, taking a huge swig. Then she cast about, as if she might be being watched. "Staff, Daphne, where are the staff?"

"Sandra's in Slough," I replied. "Her sister's due any minute and it's Brian's weekend off — golf in Ireland I think."

"Is that it?" She appeared aghast. "Just the two of them? This place is vast, how do you manage?" She looked round again, eyebrows fixed firmly skyward. "You don't want to be too relaxed about these things you know." And she actually ran her perfect manicure — remarkable considering how 'hands on' she always declared herself — along a shelf, checking for dust. "If you're paying them to do a job, Daphne, they really ought to do it … do something?" She trailed off the last bit, as if just thinking about what my staff didn't do was exhausting.

I changed the subject, saying I thought she'd lost weight, meaning it as a compliment.

"Don't be ridiculous. Been the same weight since

I was eighteen, never put on or taken off an ounce. Daddy's pointers were always jolly glad of it too." A nod to her glory days as the best female jockey the shires had ever seen. Celia was always rather good at anything she put her hand to. A bit of an extremist though, if I'm honest, but I wouldn't dream of saying that to Celia, whose mantra was "If a job's worth doing … blah … blah."

She *was* thin though, so I asked her to stay to supper more for the company than to feed her up, and although too much time with Celia could drive me to distraction, Charles was away again and she seemed more out of sorts than usual. She didn't even complain about my overcooked lasagne, polishing it off with a bottle of Chianti, after which I insisted she stay. She seemed grateful to wobble up to a guest room with a cognac and the newspaper.

It was only after she had gone to bed that I realised I had no idea why she had tipped up out of the blue. We didn't talk about anything in particular, beyond catching up on mutual friends, films and plays she had seen – she never could bear to miss the latest this or that — and then she had her usual moan about Westminster, complaining bitterly about some change to the law I rarely understood, whichever party was in charge. Although she did say something I thought was a bit strange. She asked if I minded not having children. We'd been talking about Sandra's sister's seeming unerring ability to "breed annually", as she put it, and how on earth did they manage? I had never been particularly bothered about babies and she wondered if it stung having to leave the whole estate to a distant relative — the title, the lot.

I said of course not. I'd be dead and if Charles was left behind, he'd be perfectly happy pootling about with the heir — currently a Canadian property developer – who wasn't in the best of health by all accounts.

"I think it's tragic the line will be broken," she said, misty-eyed with drink. "Heart-breaking you're the only one of you … only one of you left in the world."

I told her I rather liked being the only one, unique if you like, but she uncharacteristically squeezed my hand.

"We were left with too much responsibility, you and I. Too much to try to hold on to. People think living in these glorious old houses is wonderful, but it's such hard work. Sometimes I find myself despairing," she said, her still pretty mouth turned down.

I was shocked. I'd never heard her say such a thing. Celia of all people, the marker by which everyone set their highest standard. I didn't know what to say, so we just sat together in silence, the fire dying and the night closing in. I must have dozed off, because when I awakened her chair was vacant.

By the time I stumbled downstairs to let the dogs out next morning, Celia had gone, but not before scribbling a note of thanks and a strangely cryptic message asking me to meet her in town the following Friday, at the British Museum of all places. I checked trains and the diary. I don't know why because I never put anything in it, and with everyone still away made my mind up to go; I hadn't been to town in an age.

She was gazing into a sarcophagus when I came up behind her, making her jump, which made me laugh and her angry, so no change there then.

"Really, Daphne grow up," she sniped, and grabbing my elbow wheeled me off to the coffee shop. That's when she told me she was going to Australia. She wasn't sure for how long but could I loan her a bit of cash as everything was tied up in this and that and she needed to go right now — something about an old aunt in the Outback. All news to me, but I agreed because Celia had never asked me for anything ever and her eyes were burning into me like pokers and she looked urgent and rather frightened. So we went straight to Barclays on the Strand and the deed was done.

It was Charles who broke the news of her demise. She'd passed away peacefully in a private hospice, funeral all arranged, everything paid for. It was Lucinda who had phoned. I was in the garden, sitting on a bench looking at the flowers Celia had disparaged.

"She never made it to Australia then?" I said when I realised what he had said.

"Australia?" Charles was shocked, "Really?"

"She said that's why she needed the money."

"You gave her money? When? How much?"

"Just a couple of grand, a few weeks ago. She said she was going to Australia. Something about an aunt in the Outback."

Charles threw his eyes skyward and left me to my begonias, and then I remembered the missing emerald and how lots of things had changed for Celia recently: the vintage Daimler gone, the horses sold, a couple of paintings sent to be restored, the spaces on the wall still empty.

Celia had always been a stickler for tradition, slavishly maintaining an extravagant and rather old-fashioned lifestyle, long after her parents had gone. Mind you, the Barrington-Symthes always had pots of money, stocks and shares all over the place, or so I was given to believe. Unlike Charles and I with a huge, rambling house we couldn't afford to maintain these days. But it suited us, and Charles said the National Trust would snap our hands off if we only said the word. Which, of course, we never would.

I stared unseeing at the flowers, recalling the last

time I'd seen her, her thinness, her eyes pleading and of all the things I remembered about her, it was her unconcealed envy of something over which I had no control and really couldn't care less about. I could hear her now.

"We're just blow-ins compared with your lot, Daphne. We've only been around a few hundred years if that. Your family has been here forever — such a lineage, remarkable really." She would stand, hands thrust into her coat pockets, gazing out over the lake to the ruined castle we played in as children. "But none of it matters to you does it? What a waste, what an absolute, criminal waste."

I shrugged at her jibes, and honestly did any of it matter really? I've always thought of myself as a bit of an old hippy — you know, live and let live, do the best you can while you're on the planet, then shuffle off, no harm done. I didn't think anybody really cared about all that stuff anymore. But Celia did, so it seemed.

On the morning of her funeral I was surprised by the large display of roses Charles insisted we place on the coffin — not our roses but cream ones from a very smart florist in the high street. And as Celia had no family to speak of, I knew she would appreciate the gesture, though goodness knows if the species was appropriate, she could be so picky.

And then the biggest shock of all: the will and indeed, the emerald, as it transpired the only remaining item of the Barrington-Smythe treasure-trove — the rest of it sold, years ago. Rumour had it the emerald had been recently retrieved from a stay at a pawn-broker in Hatton Garden and not for the first time either. Imagine my surprise to discover Celia had left it to me.

'My dearest friend,' said the note, written in her tight little hand. 'I know this doesn't matter a jot to you, which is why I want you to have it. Wear it often and think of me from time to time.' Suddenly overcome, I splodged the rest of the writing away with my tears.

"Don't tell me I'm going to have to look at that bloody thing every morning over breakfast!" Charles had declared, quite ferociously for him. But I ignored his protests, and besides, we never had breakfast together anyway.

Celia did have the last laugh though, and I have to say, I laughed with her, when many years later, having some pieces valued, a red-faced insurance clerk revealed the emerald was a complete and utter fake and the diamonds only paste. My much admired inherited jewel was a dud.

"Well, you great big fraud," I told the gem, swearing the young man to secrecy as I placed it firmly back on my finger. "You're just for show. Talk about fur coat and no knickers!" Another of Celia's favourite sayings. And just like her, I never take it off — even when I'm gardening or making my trade mark potato salad, so there!

End

She Never Stops at Traffic Lights

She never stops at traffic lights,
Those pretties in the road,
Surely they're for someone else,
Who's needing to be slowed?

She never stops at traffic lights,
Full stops, a challenge, too.
She has so much to see and hear,
And such a lot to do.

Her diary's always bursting full,
With dates for this and that,
There's stuff to do, most every day,
There's just one out, that's flat!

She couldn't stop at traffic lights,
Nor barely makes a plane.
Just hoping that the world will wait,
With minutes yet to gain.

She knows not where the brake is,
She doesn't have the time.
She's charging through this race called life,
So speedy, it's a crime.

Yet take her to the seaside,
And plonk her by the shore.
She'll sit and sit for hours,
She wants for nothing more.

She knows not what the time is,
She cares not for the tides,
They'll come and go as suits them,
With nothing else besides.

She never stops for traffic lights,
She must know it's a crime.
But when she sees the ocean break,
What else is there but time?

A Married Man

"What's yours like?" Gina asked, expertly reapplying lipstick as her mouth moved.

"He seems very nice," her companion said, drying her hands carefully as Gina wriggled even closer to the mirror.

"Has he offered you a lift home?" The door opened and the blast of pulsating music almost drowned out the end of the question. Gina frowned distractedly at the reflection of a girl disappearing into a cubicle. She had been trying to concentrate on her eyelashes.

"No. But I … wouldn't. Why, are you going home with yours?" her friend asked, wide-eyed.

"Eve, how could you even suggest such a thing!" gasped Gina, batting her super-lashed lids. Her expression changed. "Yeah, if I can swing it. I think he looks like an older Richard Gere, don't you?"

"Richard Gere's pretty old already," Eve ventured,

smoothing her hair a little.

"Now, now, cheeky," Gina said, trying out her 'winning smile' before snapping her bag shut.

Eve was smoothing down her hair again, this time in the passenger mirror of his car. Eve liked everything neat and tidy. Her short blonde bob always looked immaculate, but her hands were hot and her throat felt dry. Chatting most of the evening with the handsome, very attentive stranger had perked her up no end, and for some reason, probably the cocktails, she had been feeling unusually confident. Now all the bubbly confidence had ebbed away and she was, despite her bland expression, desperately trying to imagine what Gina would do in this situation. She would probably smile alluringly, say something witty, if a little lewd, and kiss him. Then she would calmly invite him in for coffee with that tell-tale wicked gleam in her huge hazel eyes and he would know exactly what she meant and there would be no need for words or explanations or nervousness. Eve wished she were more like Gina.

He drank the coffee gratefully and then, reaching across the kitchen table in her tiny, tidy flat he took her hand and smiled at her.

"You're a lovely girl, Eve," he said, his soft Yorkshire accent making her shiver. "A really lovely girl."

She wanted to ask if she would see him again, if he'd call, make a date. Gina had warned it was always best to find out where you stood. It spared all that mooning around, longing and aching and hoping. And it meant you could get out as soon as possible and start looking for a replacement if things were to be that way. No point in wasting any more time. No one was getting any younger. Despite her outward frivolity, Gina was extremely practically minded when it came to men.

He struggled into his trousers and she sat up in bed watching him, stifling a giggle as he hopped around her Laura Ashley bedroom in his socks. But she didn't speak, she just looked hopeful.

He asked for her telephone number and she wrote it out carefully on a page of the pad she kept by the bed for messages. She didn't ask why he wanted it or when he might use it, she just kissed him gently before he clambered downstairs and out into the dawn.

They sat opposite each other in the canteen. It was one of their weeks for being on duty together. Eve was thinking how unfair it was that the stark nurse's uniform always managed to transform Gina into a real beauty, bringing out her finer points, giving her poise and an aura of serenity.

The contrast between her call-girl cum dancing queen jumble of street clothes could not be more startling. This was probably why none of the young doctors she had dated in the past bothered to take the relationship further than a couple of cheap nights out and a bit of slap and tickle afterwards, mused Eve. Though Gina was very open about the fact she liked men and lots of sex, she considered it dishonest to change her off-duty image to ensnare a potential husband.

Eve would have liked to have been able to change, just a little bit, if she could. She knew her uniform did nothing for her physically, she just seemed to disappear inside it. But it did give her something very important – confidence — and this was vital to Eve because her work was the only thing in her life that had ever given her confidence. Until now anyway. Until Rick.

"Well, quite the steady boyfriend then isn't he?" Gina said, slightly put out, but at the same time pleased for her small, mousey friend.

Eve stirred her coffee, then Gina's, helpfully.

"I wouldn't say that," she replied.

"We haven't been out together for over a month now," Gina whined, who valued Eve's friendship more than most people imagined, including Eve. "You're always waiting in for Rick. Why can't you make the arrangements for a change?"

Eve's fingers tightened around her coffee cup. She leaned conspiratorially across the table towards Gina, pale eyes glancing quickly around the room.

"It's very difficult," she hissed, turning pink. "You see, he's married."

The night he told her was like a vivid, recurring nightmare. Every time she closed her eyes, even during the day, on the ward, she could see him as he sat there. Brow furrowed, mouth grim, his hand with the gold wedding band placed in the palm outstretched towards her. It seemed to glint in the candlelight, defying her, unafraid.

"That's why I brought you here tonight, Eve. Because I can't deceive you anymore. And now you know, well, I can understand you sending me packing. That's why I thought a candlelit dinner, good wine, soft music … oh, I don't know, it seems the only way to say farewell to someone as sweet and lovely as you, my darling, my Evie." His eyes glistened.

She was plunged into despair, and yet she felt she had never loved him more than at that moment, when he bared his soul and tried to tell her how impossible their love was.

She had held him tightly that night, kissing him passionately and making love with a ferocity that surprised him. Tonight should have been filled with tears and recriminations, angry words and sad inevitable goodbyes. Not lust and passion and fervour. Yet these were the emotions she wanted him to see in her eyes. Those soft, pale eyes, now hard and fierce and determined.

Things weren't going to plan, Rick decided. Instead of crumbling as he had expected, she had become firm and resolute. No matter how often he cancelled dates, failed to turn up or didn't bother to phone, she would be waiting, unreproachful, waiting to give him sex and food and warmth whenever he ran out of alternatives.

He told her he had three children. He couldn't possibly leave them, not yet, perhaps never — he adored them. He told her he still slept with his wife. She was a demanding woman. She would suspect if he didn't, maybe leave him and take his beloved children. But none of this mattered to Eve; she never even flinched. She just smiled and said she understood, stroking his hair and kissing his forehead.

"I thought once you told them you were married they dropped you like a hot brick?" queried Clive, leaning against the water cooler.

"They usually do, that's why I always pick the nice, shy type. The ones looking for someone to settle down with. The type that is usually so upset and disgusted at being involved with a married man they're almost glad to see the back of me." Rick fingered the gold wedding band he carried in his pocket. He was annoyed that things weren't working out this time, not going to plan at all.

"Go on Brenda, please," Rick pleaded charmingly. "It's the only way, honestly. I wouldn't ask but I have to break free, let the poor girl go once and for all."

Brenda was weakening. His big brown eyes and endearing smile were bringing pressure to bear. She didn't really want to telephone this 'poor girl' and pretend to be Rick's wife. It wouldn't be the first time he had used her to help get him out of some sort of emotional tangle or other. But he was so handsome and her job in accounts so tedious, a little bit of drama might help the day along.

"Oh, all right then, just this once. But I pity the poor woman who does marry you, honest I do. Far too good at getting other people to do your dirty work, always have been." Brenda shook her head, smiling. Rick grinned back, he looked relieved. The end was in sight.

Eve was distraught after the phone call. Distraught and upset, but upset for Rick not herself. That cruel, heartless bitch of a woman, to threaten her like that, to threaten Rick's happiness and that of their three children. She just couldn't believe it — how anybody could be so wicked, so selfish!

Yet Eve knew she would do it — that woman would do what she said. She would take the children, all the money from the joint account, the car, and disappear – Rick would never see her or the children again. The woman had told Eve that she had to stop seeing him, she just had to; the children were everything to Rick, surely Eve must know that? If she wanted him on those terms, the woman said, she could have him, because losing the children would turn Rick into a shell, a shell of his former self. If she could live with that, she could have him.

Eve knew what she must do; she had given it considerable thought. Rick loved her, she was sure of that, and what they had together had been very special. But now it must end and she must end it. It must be final and complete, for Rick's sake, for the sake of those beautiful little children. There was no point in just saying that it was over, Rick loved her too much to let things go at that. He would try to see her again, jeopardise their futures, the happiness of all concerned. No, she must remove temptation once and for all. She had to go where there was no chance he could find her, get to her. She knew what she had to do.

She had just returned from her morning shift at the hospital when the phone rang. It was Rick.

"My wife, she knows about us. She said she's spoken to you, told you to stop seeing me. She'll take the children away. Oh, Eve, what are we going to do? Don't say it's over between us … I can't bear it … I don't think I can go on."

"I know darling, but it really is for the best." She was explaining. "I love you, I always will, but it is over for us. We'll never see each other again, you understand? Say that you understand." She was crying.

"Yes," — he gave a dramatic sigh — "I understand."

After she replaced the receiver, Eve took the envelope containing the pills from the pocket of her uniform. She swallowed them down with two large tumblers of Scotch, grimacing as she did. Then she lay down on the bed she had shared in love with her darling Rick and closed her eyes as the warmth of the whisky filled her stomach and the effect of the cocktail made her head spin. She left no note, no message, nothing to incriminate him. But he would know, know what she had done for him, his happiness and their love.

Rick gave Brenda and Clive the thumbs-up sign as he came out of the office. Brenda smiled at him, giving him a flirtatious glance.

"A free man again?" she said, the hope in her voice barely disguised.

Clive was not impressed.

"Why don't you just break it off like any normal fella?" he asked, shaking his head."Getting Brenda to do your dirty work for you … telling lies and pretending. It's a real coward's way out if you ask me."

"Not at all, it's best this way. No one gets hurt really. They give me up because it's the honourable thing to do – they feel kind of good about it. They don't know that it's me calling it a day — leaves their pride intact, see." Rick grinned his endearing grin at them both.

"Well, I think you must get some kind of perverse pleasure out of all the play-acting," sniped Clive, going back to his work huffily.

"It's only a bit of fun. What harm can it do?" said Rick, laughing, unrepentant as he casually flicked the wedding band into the air, catching it in the palm of his hand.

End

SOUTHSANDS SEPTEMBER

We sat and ate and were replete,
In all our senses, quite complete.
The taste of food fresh from the sea,
The sweetness of the vine
And thee.

A view of fields that grazed the sky,
Yet fell to shores before our eye,
A swirl of blue, a lush of green
And every hue shone in between.

A day touched by a hint of sun
Then tinged with autumn just begun,
The whisper of the sea's sails sigh,
As summer says a soft goodbye.

The Retiring Type

From: Justin Jason Vale, Theatrical Agent (retired)
Date: Thur 2 Dec 2010
Email to: Isobel Stewart DBE
Subject: The Retiring Type

Dearest Isobel

I have devastating news. Gertrude has announced her retirement. I pretended to ignore it, pay it no heed whatsoever, feigned the words had not been uttered, but today it arrived by post, a proper letter in an envelope, giving my full title and address and stating her intention to leave my employ at the end of the month.

I was surprised to say the least. To emphasise the point, she'd mailed the missive first class and propped it in full view against my boiled egg, surely an irrefutable sign of her commitment to the decision. I mean, we all know she has no recognised means of pecuniary support, being the worst nurse in the world! Supposedly a 'retrained psychiatric' — more like retarded psychotic — but she seems determined this time.

I'm concerned though. Hers is a chequered career as we both know. Remember when she tried to supplement her income with part-time pole dancing up at the Crushed Velvet Club and it did not suit one iota? Ended up with sciatica all down one side — and addicted to co-codamol by the end of it — and I'm the one supposedly on medication. Contrary to what she would have us believe, I don't think she ever made the grade as an understudy for Pans People, but I'd never say as much, of course.

And let's not forget the time she tried a stint at St Winifred the Wanderer Infants and Crèche. Thought she could pull in a shift while I had my afternoon nap, but I spotted her stirring diazepam into my elevenses hoping I would nod off before *The World at One*, just so she could totter down the high street and poison the poor little darlings from depraved homes who had to eat school dinners. Anyway, when they checked her references and more of her past was revealed — nothing official of course — I knew her days as a dinner lady were numbered.

She said she was going to haul them over the coals for racial prejudice, you'll recall, when I found her with her mascara streaked in the back pantry, mixing one of her knock out Martinis to steady her nerves. But we all know she's from Spalding and the skin discolouration is the result of regular visits to the Hollywood Boulevard Tanning Emporium attached to Zoe Tilbury's garage extension. And before you ask, I don't think she ever got planning permission, but when one's brother's an MP, say no more.

Anyway, must dash. The rattle of keys is on the stair, I'll keep you posted.

Yours, J.

From: Isobel
Date: Fri, 3 Dec 2010
To: Justin
Subject: A replacement

Justin

Bound to be a shock, but Gertrude has been with you for over twenty years. She'll be sixty five soon, time to move on. Have you started to look for a replacement? Get in touch with an agency soonest and do check the references.

Regards, Isobel.

From: Justin Jason Vale
Date: Sat, 4 Dec 2010
To: Isobel Stewart
Subject: Midlife crisis

Dear Isobel

Gertrude's certainly convincing, I'll give her that. Started removing the collection of ensembles stored in the attic, sorting things into piles: vintage (mothballed); classic (early M&S) and utilitarian; (namely, anything she's been wearing during daylight hours for the past decade). The hatboxes followed: one home to an abandoned bird's nest, another the festering fox fur turban and the third a hiding place for a wilted trilby which she now seems loathe to remove. Been wearing it for three days with that soulful look in her eye.

I think it's a midlife crisis and told her so last evening after she delivered, to my horror, a measly measure of cognac — I always take port after venison. She's also started handing me After Eights, well before seven, but I'd made the mistake of letting it go unchallenged and now look where we are.

Anyway she was furious. Flounced out saying she was nowhere near mid-life or indeed a crisis, telling me I was well able to get up and pour my own drinks, open my own chocolates and, come to that, look after myself

– more or less decrying the fact I have been cripplingly ill and housebound for years. In one sentence she managed to sweep my entire medical history under the carpet. Not that she's ever done any sweeping, or even knows where the hoover lives. I was shell-shocked, to say the least, and had to drink the cognac anyway.

I decided to leave the aforementioned diatribe un-remarked, and at cocoa time I asked if a little trip to Covent Garden might cheer her up — a show perhaps, cocktails with some of the old troupe?

Bit my face off. Did I not recall she was barred from the Master Cutler? Recounting the time we took the 9.06 from Loughborough and reaching for my hip flask she flashed a little too much thigh and lace suspender at the waiter in first class, who in a spasm of excitement, grabbed the communication cord. We were thrown into chaos before being forced to disembark at Market Harborough. Thereby depriving us of her aisle-long tango with the nice lady who pilots the tea trolley from Kettering, such a shame as Kettering always needs a little livening, I'm sure you'll agree.

So I decided to keep the peace and let the hare sit, gently offering Ronald and the Range Rover to help deliver her redundant gear to the charity shop. She snapped again, declaring she was retiring, not retreating to a nunnery and her frocks and furs would be called back into commission once she lost a few pounds and had her hair done. Of course, we all know it's a wig, but I kept my counsel.

Have you heard a word? She always speaks so highly of you.

I must away now. I can hear the dogs returned from their walk. They make such a fuss of me when they get back — always seem relieved she hasn't skinned them to turn them into a coat.

Fondest, J.

From: Isobel
Date: Sun, 5 Dec 2010
To: Justin
Subject: Have you tried the Internet?

Justin

It appears Gertrude's mind is made up. Time is pressing and you must find a replacement. Make sure someone is with you when you interview the candidates. Probably best not to ask them to do a turn. I know you love a good audition but it's their care skills you're really interested in.

Isobel

From: Justin Jason Vale
Date: Tue, 7 Dec 2010
To: Isobel Stewart
Subject: Bribery and corruption

Seeking your guidance dear friend

Well, it's gone from bad to worse. In a fit of pique, Gertrude's taken all her homemade meals out of the freezer to defrost. I tried to look suitably perplexed but she really is the most filthy cook, so was looking forward to restocking from Waitrose, when she spotted the latest edition of *The Lady* and flew into a rage, saying I couldn't wait to find a replacement.

That was the straw that broke the camel's back, she said and she couldn't remain in my presence, let alone my employ, for a minute longer, and as soon as her stipend was safely in her purse, she would be gone.

As you're well aware, she's had access to all the bank accounts for years, ever since that doctor threatened to have me sectioned and she threw him the length of the drive; loyalty, and indeed a rugby tackle such as that, will never be forgotten. But it seems she is no longer the devoted, caring maid she once was. She says she wants new horizons, for goodness sake. I said she could move to the east wing … lovely horizon from there on a good day.

I even suggested she look up some old friends, re-establish a bit of a social life, although I've maintained my ban on that Malcolm Greenwich-Browne! You remember, the defrocked vicar from the next parish? He always had a stash of coke for dress rehearsals when Gertrude was in his beastly Alternative Choir.

I swore if I had to sit through another rehearsal of 'I Will Survive' I'd stick candle wax in my ears and stand in the pulpit with my thermal vest pulled over my head and see how they liked it! Sadly, it was the only song the menopausal matrons could remember all the way through, screeching it out like banshees while Cyril the gay curate played something by Queen on the organ.

I always ended up asking if there was an alternative to the 'Alternative', and if so, could someone rush it round to the vestry and be quick about it. Mind you, the coke was a blessing in some ways. Didn't help with remembering lyrics but meant they didn't give a damn about what they'd forgotten. But she told me she wasn't bothered about Malcolm and had new fish to fry. I gave up, but I did ask her to fry the fish while I'm at the clinic. Can't stand the smell.

Anyway, she's confirmed her date of departure, posted it on the notice-board in the village hall and sent flowers to Grenville, the sub-post-master who, I tried to point out, was never as discreet as she thought — we all knew where the DVDs came from.

Then, to crown it all, she cancelled my birthday hamper from Fortnum and Mason, the only gift she ever bestows, even though I know I pay for it because I saw it on the bank statement.

In desperation, I tried a charm offensive with a glass of Bollinger and a sliver of smoked salmon, but the tray was left untouched outside her door. In fact, I almost think she spent the whole evening elsewhere.

And please don't complain that I have done nothing. I did click a button called 'Help' on the computer but it only threw up more questions. Help yourself, was Gertrude's retort when I mutely asked if she could assist. The last I heard was a door slam. In fact, it's all gone very quiet.

Your, now rather worried comrade, Justin

From: Justin Jason Value
Date: Wed, 8 Dec 2010
To: Isobel Stewart
Subject: Help urgently required

Isobel, Isobel, where for art thou?

It's dire here, dear friend. The biker – you remember, Gertrude's erstwhile paramour — has reappeared, ninety if he's a day, couple of grey strands in a pony-tail, earrings and a tattoo declaring I Luv Sue. Don't think he has enough skin left to delete Sue and insert Gertrude, and she won't be Gertie for love nor money.

Speaking of which, she informs me she has acquired a new, less stressful position to cushion the financial embarrassment of her change in career, and the leather-clad lovey, whose stage name is Eric Derrick — only been in an ad for nappy liners as far as I can tell — is whisking her away to take up her internment with a dear lady north of the border — older than I but less infirm I'm told.

I'm put out, put upon and ready to be put down. The latter will be required sooner rather than later, according to Gertrude, who has demanded her tiara out of the safe, being the only key I still withhold. And so I fear the threat to leave me has become a promise and the promise will be kept. Have you not heard a thing? I am at my wits' end.

I'm so sorry, dearest Isobel. I've asked nothing of your circumstances? How are you faring after the operation? Weren't you looking for someone to help with one or two chores around the Scottish estate? How did your endeavours transpire?

Whatever you do, don't let on you've plenty of room for collections of pantomime dame gowns, tattered hat boxes and a vintage, albeit newly acquired Norton, will you? Goodness knows if she heads north of the border with her new beloved they might even swing by and I know you'd love a bit of company, someone to share memories of the good old days treading the boards, but you're so nice you'd never get rid of them – mark my words.

Your favourite theatrical agent, Justin. X

End

Middle-Aged Crush

I seem to have a crashing crush,
It hit me in a raging rush,
It's on a man who's very young,
The same age as my youngest son!

Hot flushes aren't the menopause.
The palpitations he can cause,
Just standing very close to me,
Is that knocking sound my knee?

A fingernail along my spine,
Remembered from another time,
Those goose-bumps and the heat within
Are imaginings that I'm with him.

The yearning pain I now endure
Must wait, until they find a cure,
This crashing crush will pass, I bet.
But please not now, and not just yet.

A Visit at Christmas

"No, not today," she said too quickly, desperately trying to remain calm. Mr Oswald shook his head gently. "We must run further tests as soon as possible. To wait with this sort of indication would be folly, Mrs Hunter."

"The day after, then. Give me one more day." She was pleading.

"It's not what I give you, Mrs Hunter but what you give yourself," he said, frowning slightly. "And with Christmas almost upon us, if anything needs urgent attention I would prefer to be on hand to see to things myself." He closed her file on his desk. "Of course, my colleagues are equally experienced …"

"Tomorrow. I'll be at the hospital tomorrow. First thing, I promise."

The consultant shrugged. The bizarre values of women never ceased to amaze him. She probably had some shopping to complete or a hair appointment. But she was a longstanding patient and they had fought such battles before. He gave her one of his reassuring smiles as he showed her out. He hoped this time she had someone to lean on. In all the years he had known her she had only ever attended appointments alone.

She was of little use in the office that day. Half her mind worried about the tests and possible outcome, while the other half looked excitedly forward to the evening which lay ahead.

The bodies bustled by, bulky in layers and overcoats. Bags bumped bags as she scanned faces beneath hats, swathed in scarfs, anxiously searching. He might not come. He hadn't once before, he had missed the train and couldn't reach her. The weather had turned and he had turned back. He might not come this time, it had been so long.

And then she saw him, standing stock still amid the blur of hurry, watching her, smiling as he brushed strands of dark hair from bright happy eyes. He seemed to shine like a beacon against the dull backdrop of the grey station and taupe travellers. Her heart leapt; he had come.

Side-stepping commuters, he raced towards her, and they embraced warmly, patting each other with gloved hands and much smiling.

"You look good," she beamed.

"You too. I see you're still managing to keep the wrinkles at bay." He took her arm.

"Time will tell on you too, young man, and don't come looking to borrow the night cream when it does," she said grinning as she squeezed his arm.

His luggage was meagre, a dishevelled backpack and battered leather bag slung across broad shoulders. Despite his years he looked like a student with spectacles and stubbly chin — faded jeans and rugby shirts still the mainstay of his wardrobe. He had made one concession to the occasion, she noticed. His hair was professionally cut, an attempt at taming the wild waves she adored, but it suited him, highlighting his cheekbones, the determined chin. Still a good-looking devil, she thought, already enjoying being with him.

He laughed when they reached her car. "Do they give you a new one when the old one gets dirty?"

"If the newness and opulence of my vehicle offends your socialist principles, you can always walk!" She zapped the doors.

"It'll have to do. No-one knows me around here any way." He threw his bags onto the back seat.

They chatted easily as she took the busy ring road out of the early evening city. They caught up on each other's work, ongoing projects and mutual colleagues they had known. Soon suburbia glinted cosily in the amber-tinted dusk and gardens dotted with fairy lights twinkled a welcome.

"Made any improvements to your fairy-tale castle recently?" he asked as they pulled into the drive of the large Victorian villa.

She laughed. He had always secretly admired her exquisite if rather opulent taste, teasing that her home should feature in a glossy magazine.

"No, but I've taken up the carpet in the guest suite so you'll feel more at home, and the brown rice and lentils should be done to a turn in the Aga, of course."

He ruffled her hair. "You know what I like." He had been a strident vegan in his youth, but times had changed, for them both. "No prince yet, then?" he asked, glancing up at the balcony which graced the gable end.

"Still saving for the red carpet," she replied, opening the huge hall door.

The venison casserole was delicious, the claret perfect. Piling his plate with winter crumble and brandy butter, he ate as if he were half starved. He had recently returned from aid work in Syria. She had been aware of an undercurrent of worry all the time he had been away and had almost wept with relief when she heard his voice again, saying he would be back in time for Christmas. It felt like the first time she had relaxed in months she considered, watching him pour drinks as he poured out his report. Hard news, tough times, another unwinnable war. Battles, she thought, always battles.

"Any news on the book front?" he asked, eyes searching hers. He knew how much the book meant to her and hoped, as much as she did, that one day it would take the publishing world by storm.

"Don't think it's going to make the bestseller list anytime soon, but the recycle bin is bursting with redrafts so at least it's not wasted."

"Hey, none of it is wasted. It's important to you. It's okay to be disappointed, anxious even. Your time will come." He raised his glass. "Never, never, never give up!"

"Quoting Churchill now, you *have* changed."

He shifted in his chair. "I've mellowed. So have you. In the olden days we'd have had at least three rows by now and would probably be throwing crockery." He looked at the underneath of a plate, pulling a face. "Probably not."

She took it off him and went to stack the dishwasher. He came to help.

"You know how to do this?" she asked. "You *are* moving in different circles."

He gave her a nudge. "I've learnt to cook too. I needed to, especially if I'm thinking about settling down."

She stopped what she was doing. "Seriously? Anyone I know?"

"Not especially." He walked away. "Time for some of your awful music. Which dreadful old crooner shall I select, Bryan Ferry or Elton John?"

"They call it vintage these days." She laughed, but the laugh sounded hollow. Maybe this *was* the last time he would come.

Later, in the drawing room, with coffee and cognac they were arguing — a good old fashioned row just like the old days. Politics, celebrities, movies, they debated all and everything. They disagreed, shouted each other down and mostly laughed their heads off. He rarely won. She had been his mentor, his teacher, his guide – he was still a little in awe of her, and she still wildly impressed by him.

She had taught him how to argue, think things through, reach a considered conclusion — philosophy, economics, sociology — all manner of things all those years ago, and now he had made changing the world his goal and she, to his mind anyway, had 'sold out'. A business consultant, international and award-winning, but a highly paid commercial parasite nonetheless. He had told her so, many times. They agreed to differ, but over the years their differences had lessened as their friendship blossomed, the visit before Christmas a tradition they had always tried to maintain.

"Time for bed," she said, taking glasses to the kitchen. She stopped at the worktop to clear space and, moving paperwork she spotted the note from her consultant. He had made her forget about tomorrow, her appointment.

"What's that?" He was behind her. Dropping the glasses, she sent them crashing to the floor. Absentmindedly she bent down, picking up pieces with her bare hands. He lunged at her, grabbing her wrists to roughly shake the splinters from her fingers.

"What are you doing? You could really hurt yourself doing that!"

She looked at him, bemused. She wasn't thinking. His bright eyes were shining with pain and concern. She looked down to his hands on her wrists, large man's hands holding her tiny bones and he seemed to fill the room, his presence smoothing over everything like a protective cloak. Her knees gave way and he took her in his arms.

"Come and sit down. It's just shock."

"And red wine," she said, once she found her voice again.

"Agreed, you can't take it like you used to."

She gave him a playful cuff. "I do okay."

He sat beside her. "Seriously though, what would you do if anything happened? Where's your back-up team, alone in this big house with copious amounts of red wine."

"Hey, I'm not ready for a personal alarm just yet."

"I didn't mean that." He looked into her eyes. "But you deserve to have someone special, you know."

She blinked at him. "I have boyfriends … well, men friends anyway." She had been long divorced, even before they had met and she had never wanted to marry again, her career was enough. Had been enough.

"But I mean someone permanent, someone here to care for you, love you all the time."

"Reckon I'll soon be past it, do you?"

He took her hand. "Don't be daft, but you do need someone. I mean, what if when you're older and ill there's no one to care for you …"

She swallowed hard. He didn't know about the hospital, she knew that, but it was an odd conversation for them. They always pretended everything was hunky dory, the world outside was falling apart but they were okay, their parallel lives, just fine. She knew him too well and despite a deep dread, followed her instinct.

"Have you found someone special then?"

His eyes grew soulful. She had her answer.

"Yes, I think so … I hope so. It's up to her now really."

"Well, that *is* good news," she said with a forced

enthusiasm she hoped he didn't notice. "Is she wonderful?"

"Oh yes, very."

"Well, I want you to tell me all about her ..."

He squeezed her hand. "Not now, you're tired. Another time, okay?"

"Yes, another time. I need to sleep. I've an appointment fairly early in the morning."

"Anything important?"

"No, not really but I need to be there." She kissed his cheek and, watching him climb the stairs, her heart ached.

She couldn't sleep. Whenever she closed her eyes she saw Mr Oswald's grey, emotionless face and then the dread of tomorrow morning would engulf her like a damp, muggy fog and she was cold and anxious and afraid. She must have cried out and awakened her guest, for he stood silhouetted in the doorway. She switched on the light. He was watching her, his brow furrowed with concern.

"I'm sorry, did I wake you? Some silly dream I think."

He shrugged. "I couldn't sleep. These feather quilts, hopeless when I'm only used to bare boards and newspaper." He moved towards the bed, she raised a hand in protest but he ignored it and sat down in front of her. "What's troubling you, there's been something wrong all evening?"

She tried an indulgent look. "Nothing important. Honestly, go back to bed. I don't think …"

He shook his head.

"You don't think you should tell me what's wrong? Still trying to protect me from the harsh realities of life? I think that's rather selfish."

She sat up, pulling the covers to her chest. "Selfish?"

"Yes, what does it matter that I care about you and am worried out of my mind?" He was glaring at her. "Tell me. I'm an adult. I can take it."

She turned away. She couldn't do it. She had never told anyone any of this. She couldn't share this pain with another, especially not with the only person in the world she really, truly cared about.

Grabbing her hard by the shoulders he forced her to look at him, his eyes immediately softening as he realised she was powerless and frightened, and the last thing in the world he wanted to do was to hurt her.

"Okay, have it your way," he said quietly, and then, leaning forward touched her lips gently with his. Her eyelids fluttered open, and looking up at him she saw for the very first time all the love and longing she had only ever dared hope for. Taking her in his arms, he crushed her to him and the wave of emotion that coursed through her shook her to her very core.

They made longed for, passionate love and later lay entwined, clasped tightly together. She nestled against his chest as he stroked her hair for all the world like a baby in his arms.

"I will always treasure this evening. It may be all we have," she whispered against his skin, relieved he had not noticed the lump.

He caught the meaning of her words. He too had seen the note from the oncologist, the overnight bag in the downstairs loo, but he was old enough and wise enough to play along. They kissed and she slept, though he saw dawn break with damp eyes and much worry.

He held her tightly at the station. Not the affectionate hug of the friends who had met the previous evening, but the lingering embrace of lovers, wrenched apart as lovers often are. She waved gaily as she ran to the car and swiftly shut the door to the sound of his train pulling away from the platform. His words of last night were ringing in her ears. Yes, she did deserve someone special to take care of her in her old age and whatever ill health might befall her, but she wanted someone special now, now while she was still young enough to enjoy him and he her, so that they could grow old and ill together. He was the special one. She wanted him.

Wiping her eyes, she drove off towards town.

He watched the car go and, walking briskly from the platform, dialled the number of a small hotel within walking distance of the hospital. He looked at his watch. He would be checked in, unpacked and at her bedside by the time she came round from the anaesthetic. He'd tell her then that this was the last time he would be visiting for Christmas, the last time he would be visiting ever. He was here to stay, *in sickness and in health, to love and to cherish, till death us do part.*

End

The Stag

What strength of limb and foot so fleet
Would be combined in one so sweet
The mildest eye, the gentlest look
That scans the forest, glades and brook.

A velvet muzzle, soft and moist
To nuzzle roots and shrubs of choice
Never tear at flesh or bone,
A savage nest to make your home.

Yet somehow with a force unseen
You make the glen, your realm, your scene
Within the mists and barks of time
The monarch of his world sublime.

The hunted which is stalked and caught
Yet never sought his fate's onslaught,
A delicacy your flesh to taste
Your antlers prized in pride of place.

Yet watchful at the water's edge
Your subtle rule leaves words unsaid
Though King of all the world you view,
The vanquished is the loss of you.

The Proper Thing

The boy was new to the area, so they made him go and retrieve the ball from Mrs Walsh's front garden. It was a test. The woman could be seen tidying a flowerbed beneath the front room window of the red-bricked terraced house. The ball bounced once and rolled towards her.

She looked up. The boy met her eyes and half-smiled indicating the ball. She was immediately irritated, invaded. She wanted to snap at him, scare him off so that he and the other boys would stop playing football near her neat front garden. He spoke first.

"I'm sorry to disturb you. It was an accident. But may I have our ball back?" His accent was different, well-spoken, a new boy. So charming, she thought, the little tinker. He'd already learned how to achieve with charm. He took a step closer, his face open and honest, showing no sign of fear.

"You keep your garden very nice," he said.

She sighed, the smug little chancer. "And it would be kept nicer if you and your like kept your football away from it."

"I know, I'm sorry," he replied, not sounding remotely contrite.

Suddenly furious, she lunged for the ball and threw it at him.

"Get out, get out, you cheeky little tyke," she roared. And shrugging, barely ruffled, he took the ball, skipping back to his comrades in arms, who were impressed he had survived his first encounter with 'Witchee Walsh'.

She calmed herself with a glass of sherry, watching them through her sitting room window, playing less enthusiastically now, she noticed, the new boy's encounter with her seeming to have stifled their ebullience. The cheek of him, she thought to herself. He could have been her grandson and not a lick of respect in him. The liberty he had taken addressing her as an equal. Worse, some doddering old dear he felt a need to placate, talk down to. If he had lipped her with cheek as the others had in the past she would not have been surprised, but it was the charm of him that bothered her, something invidious there, snakelike, the cobra waiting to pounce. It made her flesh crawl. She poured another glass. Oh yes, she had seen the like of him before.

She lay back against the headrest of the chair, pushing a few greying strands wearily behind her ears as she did. Had the funeral been only six short months ago? It could have been a whole lifetime past. She smiled, ruefully. And indeed it was, but someone else's lifetime, not her own.

She remembered it was the flashing of the diamonds set against the huge flat opal which attracted her first. She had always wanted a ring like that, though her reddened hands and short fingers wouldn't have quite done the gems justice. She supposed she could have one now if she wanted, what with the insurance and the other money but, it wouldn't be the same, she thought. She would only want it if Eamon bought it for her, and now, well … Eamon was gone.

A vivid recollection seared through her thoughts and she flinched. The hand to which the ring belonged was clenched, the woman's face was clenched too, clenched and white with brittle eyes. She remembered the eyes burning into hers and was puzzled, taken aback. She had seen nothing but moist, sympathetic eyes from everyone since his death. These bitter stranger's eyes held no sympathy.

She remembered searching for a familiar face when she noticed the boy standing beside the clench-faced woman. A tall boy, almost a man, about eighteen years old, Mary thought. He was dressed in black, as was the woman, but his flash of bright blond hair was brazen and his youth and vitality incongruous in the little, frozen churchyard. Mary looked kindly at him, trying to place who they were: distant relations, a business association perhaps? But she felt sure she would have known them, the brittle woman and this bright boy, here at Eamon's funeral.

Then the boy looked up from the grave directly at her and she had gasped, clutching the nearest arm to her for support. The same green eyes cracked with grey gazed into hers, and Mary understood, instantly.

She'd had quite a few visitors after the funeral, Eamon's sisters, his boss and work colleagues and what seemed like hundreds of women from the many committees, institutes and associations to which she belonged - Mary had always kept herself busy – and, of course, Miles Granger, the family solicitor. Mr and Mrs McNulty, her neighbours, had been kindness itself – for some reason she had never been able to call them by their Christian names, despite their closeness - but after a while even they called less and less.

Time passed, the visitors grew fewer and the time between visits longer, and though she wasn't sick or ailing, she did feel that after being a pillar of the community all these years it was her turn to be cosseted and attended to. But no one, it seemed, wanted to spend time with her alone. In fact, even those who called always had so little time to spend. Mary felt cheated, and so within a couple of months, having sorted Eamon's things into neat little piles, to be kept, given to charity or burned, she dressed in her second-best suit, applied a little rouge to her lips and took the short bus ride into town.

Miles made a great fuss of her, although he always did.

"Grand to see you out and about, Mary. You're looking very well, considering. And what can I do for you? There aren't any problems regarding the financial side of things are there? There shouldn't be, we had it all sorted ..." He seemed a little nervous. Mary found this fascinating. She had known Miles Granger for forty-five years, as long as she had known Eamon, and yet since Eamon's death there was a nervousness about him. Rather like the women who visited but seemed disinclined to stay, afraid to almost. Perhaps the bereaved had that effect.

"What you can do for me Miles, is give me the truth." She sat before his leather-topped desk; the huge clock on the wall above his head had a deep, echoey tick to it. "The woman at the funeral with the young man. About eighteen or twenty I'd say he was. What were they to Eamon? I've never met them. I feel sure you could throw some light on the subject."

Miles slid his bifocals along his nose.

"Woman and young man, you say. Let me see … can't recall. Oh yes, I remember, a cousin of Eamon's I seem to think. That's her son. You must have met them at weddings or funerals sometime. At least her, anyway." He agitatedly pushed some files together on his desk. "Any reason, Mary? You seem concerned?" He was talking now to fill the silence.

"Is the bewildering state of widowhood not reason enough to sound concerned?" she had replied, quite lightly given the heaviness of her heart. Miles was flustered, foostering at this desk, avoiding her eyes. Mary picked up her gloves and left. At the bus stop she took what looked like a shopping list from her bag and crossed something out.

Mary spent another two weeks at home nourishing her strength of spirit before she called upon Eamon's two younger sisters, Beatrice and Veronica. They lived near to each other in one of the better parts of town, yet their husband's careers had been no more successful than Eamon's. Perhaps their housekeeping had been more prudent but Mary could see little evidence of this. Beatrice and Veronica, and indeed the eight children they had between them, were always well fed and well dressed. Mind you, Eamon did sometimes complain of unwise investments — a bitter admission for an accountant, Mary thought.

"A cousin, yes," said Beatrice, rattling the kettle against the gas ring. "From Galway I think. Am I right, Veronica?"

"I think she came because the son was named for Eamon — family sentiment you know," Veronica, always the weaker of the two, replied in a small voice. "A little like him too, I thought." Her voice trailed off, faltering more than usual.

Having said their farewells, Mary could hear the hushed hiss of argument as she stood outside the front door making marks on her list.

The committee members waited a respectable two months before asking if Mary would consider recommencing her activities, even just a meeting a month to begin with, it would do her good, give her an interest, a purpose again. These were the reasons she had heard all her married life. When, after two years of wedded bliss there were no children, she had decided to join the Women's Association to expand her knowledge of housewifery and take her mind off her childlessness.

After five years of marriage and as many miscarriages, she considered finding employment of some kind but Eamon would not hear of it. Imagine his wife, a shop girl? For that was all she was qualified to do, and besides, that was a defeatist attitude, they would have a family yet. The medical appointments were endless.

After ten years Eamon was transferred to Dublin and lived away all week, only coming home at weekends. The committees, institutes and societies helped fill the vacuum he left each Monday morning, but it never did stop her feeling, when the house was empty, that her life was empty too.

And now they wanted her back. After years of devoted, selfless service, after all those times they had said, "Mary can do it, she has the time. I have a family to attend to." After all that giving, Mary felt she had nothing left to give. She knew the women had pitied her at first, felt sorry for her, but as time went on and tasks were left untouched, fetes and events less well organised, coffers dwindling alarmingly they needed her desperately — the one less competent than a shop girl.

"I know you mean well, ladies, but I won't be back," she said, showing them the door. "What's left of my time, I want for myself." For too long she had done what she thought was expected of Eamon's childless wife.

She searched through his things, clothes, jewellery, papers, everything, looking for something, anything that would assuage the gnawing niggle in her brain. Her task was fruitless and she was dissatisfied. It was impossible. He was an accountant, he had to have kept records. It wasn't only his profession, it was his nature.

It was a full three months after Eamon's death that Mary found herself, almost by surprise, at his grave. It was a beautiful day. Indeed all summer the sun had blazed. The earth at the grave was cracked and dry, too soon for a headstone to be placed but a simple wooden cross marked the spot. It read, 'Eamon Walsh, 1877 – 1937' plainly written by hand. Mary stared at the cross blankly and then she noticed the flowers, one last remaining wreath. Withered and tattered it lay abandoned to the left of the cross. A thought struck. She had not paid for the flowers, the wreath for Eamon's funeral; she had not settled her account. Shocked at her laxity, she hurried out of the churchyard towards town and the florist without so much as a backward glance.

Mona Murray said it didn't matter a jot, not to give it another thought, as her fat, pink fingers wrestled with the hastily written invoices impaled on a spike above the cash register — paperwork had never been the Murrays' strong point. Her plump brow furrowed as she shuffled several pieces of paper in her hand.

"That's funny, Mrs Walsh. There's more than one bill with your address on it, but some of these are very old … I don't know …"

"That's fine, Mona, I know what they are. Tot them up now and I'll pay the lot. Here, I'll take those, there's a good girl."

Mary knew that if it had been Mr Murray in the shop that day and not his daughter those old bills would never have been brought to her attention. Mary wished Michael Murray's name had been on her list so that she could have crossed it out.

The city was unfamiliar to her. She had visited it only once in her teenage years and had been so terrified of the trams, the masses of people and the roars of the street hawkers that she had never dared, or even felt inclined, to revisit Dublin in all its bawdy glory.

Leaving the train at Pearse Street, she took a taxi, telling the man the address in a loud, clear voice as if he were a foreigner. They crossed the river and Victorian glory gave way to Georgian splendour, but Mary saw none of it and though she smelled the sea and the fresh, airy boulevards of Killiney, she looked neither left nor right but stared straight ahead. Her visit had but one purpose — this was no joy ride.

The car stopped outside a four-storey, grey stone

Georgian house. A sweep of steps rising above the lower ground floor to a grand front door gave the building an air of imposition. Mary stood stock still as the taxi pulled away, suddenly cold, as if the very blood had frozen in her veins, and taking a deep breath she mounted the steps.

A tall housemaid, finely uniformed, led her through an elegant hall to a bright drawing room. The woman with the opal and diamond ring stood at the mantle. Probably twenty years Mary's junior, she was a striking beauty, regal of head and jaw, immaculately coiffured and dressed in a beautifully cut pale silk gown. Mary braced herself, pushing the flutter of panic out of her chest. She wanted to turn and run but she could not. Powerless she had no choice but to face this as if it were a bad dream she had to experience in order to embrace the new morning she had so often reassured herself would come.

"I have expected you," the woman said in a cultured voice. "How did you find us?"

"My husband, it seems was a romantic, sending you flowers, often." Mary kept her voice steady, matching her tone.

"Each weekend spent with you," the woman said, giving Mary a sour look, and then, "Forgive me, you have come a long way. Can I offer you tea, a drink, anything? I'm sorry …" The beautiful face crumpled and tears filled her eyes — she seemed to sway. Mary took a step towards her. The woman raised her hands. "I'm all right … all right honestly. Please, take a seat."

They sat perched on the edge of matching antique chairs, as the maid brought a gilt tray of tea and scones and fine china. The woman waved her away after she had poured out two cups. She looked at Mary.

"What do you know of us?" she asked.

"Nothing. I knew nothing till I saw the boy. And you, I saw the pain and anger in you and then I knew." Mary spoke plainly. No need to hide any more truths.

"But you must have known. I knew all about you. The unhappy marriage, the years of yearning for a child, how you blamed him, endlessly bemoaning your fate until he said you drove him away and he took the job in Dublin. And then how you wouldn't let him go, wouldn't separate from him and how you blackmailed him, threatening suicide, driving the poor man to his wits' end!" She stopped and looked at her hands clenched in her lap, calming herself. When she looked up at Mary her bright blue eyes were pleading. "Oh, why didn't you let him go? Not for me or him but for the boy's sake, for his son?"

Mary went to speak, to tell her she did not know the husband and wife about whom she spoke, and how could she have let the man she was married to go, when he had never asked to leave. But the woman in the pale grey dress kept talking, spilling out her thoughts, recounting memories of Eamon. How they set up home together away from people who knew them, letting all and sundry assume they were man and wife. Then the birth of their son, the gift of the opal and diamond ring to celebrate. Over twenty years they had been together — another marriage, another lifetime.

At the end of her speech, the younger woman sat, quietly sobbing, staring at an empty armchair, which must have been Eamon's. Mary had just such an armchair.

"You must have known," she said, finally composing herself. "They all knew in the end." Mary thought of her list. They all knew all right.

"I only came to say I have no claim on him. Feel free to tend the grave as you wish. I'm selling up and moving back home. There's nothing for me there, never has been, that much I know now. Let the son have his father," Mary said, rising to leave.

The woman looked anxious, as if she didn't want Mary to go, as if any fragment of Eamon was something to be clasped and cherished, even his other wife. Mary felt the other woman's grief, but did not feel it for herself. This woman had been broken by Eamon's death, left bereft and twisted with regret. If Mary had felt anything since her husband's demise it was a sense of becoming more whole, and over these last few months if Mary had come to value anything or anybody, it was herself, Mary Walsh.

She glanced around the room, the elegant home Eamon had provided for his other wife and child, his son and heir. She looked at the younger woman, with her jewellery and her good clothes; they had been well provided for - Eamon and Miles would have seen to that – and all she felt was sorry. Sorry for the woman and the child without his father's name. Sorry for Eamon, because he had never bothered to get to know her well enough to realise that she could have survived without him. She would have let him go. He was always so busy doing 'the proper thing' he rarely did anything truly right. Stupid man. Sometimes, Mary thought, being 'well-meaning' was the meanest thing of all.

"You had the best of him," she said without malice, and left, her tea untouched.

She heard the football bounce into the garden again. She went to the window and opened it. The new boy looked up and smiled. "I'm sorry, Mrs Walsh. It won't happen again, I promise."

By now, she didn't feel the least bit irritated with the child. She didn't give a damn how often they kicked the football into her front garden. They could play a five-a-side tournament in the flowerbeds for all she cared.

She closed the window and scanned the room. All

tidy and shipshape, her bags packed and by the door. She checked her watch: half an hour till the car came. Deciding to pour herself one last sherry, she slipped her hand into her coat pocket to leave the back-door key on the shelf and pulled out a sheet of paper, neatly folded. She opened it to find a list of names, people she had known all her married life, all the time she had lived there, in her small town house with the neat front garden. There was a straight black line through each and every name listed.

Mary screwed the piece of paper up and threw it in the bin, drank her sherry and put on her hat. She would wait outside for the car; it was a fine day. The lads might even let her have a little kick of that ball before she left. The neighbours' curtains would twitch at that all right.

End

The Hollow Heart

How heavy hangs a heart that is just hollow?
How filled with lead the heart that knows
no air?
It cannot lift with love when spies a loved one.
It cannot miss a beat with love to share.

The hollow heart just echoes with its longing
Without the job of love to keep it sane.
The hollow heart waits unfulfilled and wanting,
Without the strength to even feel its pain.

What hollow heart could burst with love
unbounded?
If the door was opened, just an inch.
And love, like light could flood its empty
chambers
And thus fulfilled the heart would never
flinch.

The door to love stands proud and ever open.
The key's been found and bravely flung away.
The hollow heart has found its only purpose
And beats with joy … for love has found a
way.

A Change of Heart

Sometimes a heart will tell,
The keeper of the well,
That wishes have come true,
There's nothing left to do.

But though these words are said,
There's something in the head,
That's not all as it seems,
For locked away are dreams,
And further depths to find,
Of heart and soul and mind.

Still richer veins lie deep,
Within the spirit's keep,
And mining there will show,
There's still more love to grow.

As loyalty and faith,
Humility and grace,
Such solid virtues true,
Will change the rosy hue,

Of love's first lustful charm,
To solid, granite calm,

That forms a bed of rock,
Withstanding every shock,

So nought is torn apart,
Thus turns the change of heart.

Secrets

You know I have a secret, it lies behind my eyes,
You see it clouds my history like dark, satanic skies.

My secret seeps into my dreams, creeps up while I'm awake,
My secret's like a torrid thirst, impossible to slake.

It's woven through my psyche, it's layered in my soul,
It sits in my subconscious and burrows like a mole.

My secret is the minefield, I tiptoe through at night,
Terrified the dawn will break and it becomes alight.

My secret's at the heart of me, a silent constant beat.
My secret leaves me cold with fear, yet scorched with livid heat.

But everyone has secrets, their size and scale unknown.
They lurk in shadowed corners of everybody's home.

And sometimes secrets shrivel up, they disappear like dust
And fade into the nothingness, as many secrets must.

Yet special secrets, some at least, need to be set free,
Especially when my secret is, my secret love for thee.

Acknowledgements

Creating a book is always a team effort, even people a writer meets who influence a story or a character are part of the team – a secret team in my case. Elements of this project have been bubbling on the back burner for many, many years and some of it is as fresh as this morning! I would like to thank everyone who has helped bring it to fruition, I could not have done it without you.

My grateful thanks go to my mother Marion Wrafter for her love of short stories and remembering my early ones in such detail I just had to dig them out, my amazing and talented sister, Reta Wrafter for the original cover artwork, my brilliant brother-in-law, John Reddy for design, my mentor, the historical novelist, June Tate who liked the stories enough to encourage me to publish, copy editor Richard Sheehan who helped knock them into shape, formatter and technical guru Sarah Houldcroft who turned it all into a book, my literary agent, Lisa Eveleigh who encouraged me to 'get on with it' as soon as she heard the title, my friends and supporters in the Romantic Novelists' Association and especially the New Romantics Press, June Kearns, Mags Cullingford and my special writing buddy Lizzie Lamb, for waving the flag and generously giving masses of unseen help, my dear colleague Natalie Keene, always at my back making sure the spinning plates don't drop and finally my superstar, Jonathan Vaughan, whose input and advice has been immeasurable regarding this project, even down to re-reading screwed up bits of paper and surreptitiously putting them back on my desk – thanks for believing, always.

This book is dedicated to Harry

PS: I would like it on record that I am constantly bemused, flattered and sometimes even overwhelmed when people write, email or just stop to chat about my books, wherever I am, be it the UK, Ireland or even Lanzarote … I am hugely grateful, you have no idea how much it means, so thank you, all of you.

About the Author

Adrienne Vaughan is a born storyteller and as soon as she could pick up a pen she started writing them down. It came as no surprise she wanted to be a journalist and dived headfirst into her career after graduating from the Dublin College of Journalism.

Today, she is a journalist and author having recently completed her fourth novel *Scandal of the Seahorse Hotel* to be published late 2017. In the meantime this eclectic selection of short stories and poems will surprise and enthral her many fans, as the myriad of styles and content clearly spotlights a very talented, highly captivating writer who has been compared to many, yet remains – in what is a very crowded marketplace – impressively unique.

Adrienne lives in rural Leicestershire with her husband Jonathan, cocker spaniels, Winston and Wellington and a rescue cat called Agatha Christie. She still, and always will, harbour a burning ambition to be a Bond Girl!

www.adriennevaughan.com
@adrienneauthor

www.newromanticspress.com

20259548R00112

Printed in Great Britain
by Amazon